# UNREPORTABLE EVENT

A NOVEL BY

DAVID WILLIAM KUNZ, MD

Copyright © 2024, David William Kunz, MD
Perisseia Press
All rights reserved.

ISBN: 979-8-9911734-0-7

Produced by Publish Pros | publishpros.com

This book is a work of fiction. Any references to historical events, real people, or real places are used fictitiously. Other names, characters and events are products of the author's imagination and any resemblance to actual events or places or persons, living or dead, is entirely coincidental.

# WHAT IS TRUTH?

The federal medical authorities have established a standard procedure by which adverse medical outcomes are reported to and recorded by agencies like the FDA. These events may be due to the poor design of a medical instrument or a drug. They might be due to operator error, overt negligence, or any one of myriad causes.

So, if a drug, medical instrument, or clinical procedure appears to an educated observer to have contributed to an adverse outcome, he or she can submit a record of this occurrence to the government via a number of standard procedures and forms. This constitutes a "reportable event" or "adverse outcome." If enough reports are received to raise suspicion, a formal investigation may be launched.

The narrative that follows documents one such "event," one that received no "official" explanation.

# 24 ANNO DANNY (A.D.)[1]

On the outskirts of Moscow there loomed a gray steel and glass building. It was a forbidding fortress, austere even by 1960s Soviet architectural standards. To add to its inhospitable ambiance, it was surrounded by a gray stone perimeter wall topped with concertina wire. The KGB had conducted chemical and psychological experiments there dating back to the Cold War; the American CIA had conducted the same experiments in the MK-Ultra era. The general term for such experiments was "psyops." They used psychedelics. They were trying to find the right pharmaceutical enhancement—given to special people, such as prisoners to be interrogated—in order to extract information; they also administered it to their own agents with special "abilities" to test if they could spy remotely on the enemy using ESP. The place was locked down now and appeared to all outside observers to be non-operational. The presence of sentries at the gate and the dim glow of lights on the lower level in the dead of night said otherwise.

---

[1] A.D. refers to "Anno Danny" and indicates Danny's age when the events of this narrative take place.

Dmitri flashed his credentials to the guard. "I have an important package to pick up." He was admitted.

With the fall of the Iron Curtain, the military, technical, research, and natural resources of the Empire were thrown onto the open market, ready to be exploited by those formerly on the "inside." These were the technocrats, the oligarchs, and especially former members of the FSB (formerly known as KGB) who were now able to make handsome profits from previous tools of the Cold War. Dmitri only knew that the package was to be delivered to Munich. He had his orders from the top.

# 29 A.D.

Hassan navigated his delivery van to a space next to the loading docks of Oriole Health Distribution Center located in a rural area on the outskirts of Atlanta, Georgia. It was well after midnight. He reversed the vehicle skillfully as he had done hundreds of times before, the backup warning beeping rhythmically in cadence with his heart. He had an important delivery to make. He didn't know what made this delivery different. He only knew that his Imam said it was the most important thing he could do in service to Allah and the Prophet (may his name be praised).

Hassan had sneaked in over the southern border under the radar two years before. Then he had disappeared into the fog of "We'll contact you later to go over your papers at a court hearing." He got his card. He got a good job.

He rolled his pallet up to the security door and swiped his ID card into the pad. He unloaded the shrink-wrapped cargo, which looked a little different from the other deliveries he had regularly made. He scanned the security code on it before depositing it in its assigned spot on the warehouse floor.

All was well. The pallet was marked "SAMPLES."

He would repeat this delivery many times.

# AZURE EYES (29 A.D.)

Two pairs of eyes, sparkling pools of deepest blue, were submerged in each other. Thousands of words were spoken without a single sound, except for the rhythm of two hearts and two breaths in perfect sync.

"Who are those two young trespassers over there, Sam, looking at the new doc's office?" a woman asked from across the street in her perfect Madison, Georgia, accent.

"Madge, that IS the doc, and his wife. They're just looking the place over."

"Looks like they're looking each other over if you ask me."

There they were, the two young lovers, not yet thirty years old, in a passionate, breathless, yet restrained embrace. A ponytail, a baseball cap, and two sets of running shorts and shoes were on display, adorning two trim and lithe athletic physiques. Encircled in each other's arms, they pressed breathlessly against each other. The lovers were framed by the antebellum mansion in the background with which they were both obviously enamored, although at this moment somewhat less than they were with each other.

# UNREPORTABLE EVENT

"Okay, Dr. Keene, I'll give you about two hours to stop that…"

"What?" he asked innocently.

"Oh, you know," she said, wiping the moisture off her ear in mock revulsion.

"Hmmm …" he said, leaning in again.

"Alright, there, DOCTOR KEENE. Pay attention!"

"I AM paying attention."

"To the house, you goose. I should never have encouraged you."

"Not that I needed any." He nuzzled even closer.

"Eyes front, buddy." She nudged him away gently.

"Oh, if you insist."

The object of their mutual attention, besides each other, was a beautifully restored and converted antebellum mansion in Madison, Georgia, an outlying bedroom community of Atlanta. In Georgia, there were precious few of these types of homes. Madison was blessed to have many. It was soon to be the doctor's office.

The house in view, though grand, was smaller than most of the others in the neighborhood. It lacked the tall, stately Doric columns on the exterior and the vaulted foyer showcasing a *Gone with the Wind* staircase inside. But what it lacked in extreme grandeur it more than made up for in Victorian charm.

The mansion showcased an inviting wraparound front porch featuring at least a dozen Windsor-style rocking chairs. The double front doors with elegant etched and partially frosted leaded glass panes opened into a spacious foyer that had now been converted into a reception area. Capacious antique-styled faux-leather chairs and a couple of similarly styled love seats graced the waiting room, while a couple of strategically placed rectangular coffee and corner tables rounded out the décor. The original mahogany shelves of the parlor had been perfectly restored and now were home to antique historical prints of the Madison area as well as small medical-themed statuary and other decorative touches. A Tiffany floor lamp stood proudly in the front corner of the room.

On the left side of the front foyer, a reception desk designed and built by local cabinetmakers wrapped around the foot of the staircase that ascended to the second story. (Future plans for the upstairs included more office and exam room spaces.) Extending straight ahead down the main hall for ten feet or so, the front of the desk commanded a view into the waiting area through a vaulted archway. This archway displayed lovingly restored antebellum millwork. The workers had remodeled the area behind the desk and under the stairs to contain cabinets, copiers, and other administrative necessities.

Toward the back of the house, a door had been hung. Its frame displayed the same millwork as the arched entrance to the waiting area. This door controlled access to the back office. Through it and straight down the main hall, remodelers had created other spaces: A second parlor adjacent to and behind the grand parlor at the front had been divided into two smaller offices to house the manager on one side and other administrative personnel on the other. Further down the hall, the library now served as the doctor's own office, its mahogany shelves also meticulously refinished and now housing medical books, plaques, certificates, and diplomas. This space too had been subdivided into an office and anteroom of sorts, as a place for patients to sit in private while they waited for personal consultation time with the doctor. Many other clever architectural changes transformed the whole place into a sumptuous, cozy, and inviting physician's office.

# UNREPORTABLE EVENT

The grand dining room and solarium at the back of the mansion had been divided into individual exam rooms, each with bright, cheery décor enhanced by the ample windows that each room featured. And finally, the kitchen and smaller dining area and pantry to the left of the house and behind the staircase had been converted into a laboratory, work area, and staff gathering space. Splitting the laboratory and staff break room on the left was a hallway that led out to the porte-cochere. The door at the end served as an employee entrance and as an alternate portal for patients during inclement weather. Altogether, the structural changes were masterfully accomplished, preserving the antique character of the mansion while transforming it into an ideal place for doctoring.

"The contractors are done with the front desk and reception area. We've got to get all that exam room furniture moved in tomorrow and Tuesday. First day is in a week," Kaye said.

She was such an organizer and he loved her for it. He lamented to himself that for him, everything was organized between his ears (and was subject, of course, to frequent REorganization), but his external environment, if he had anything to do with it, was usually a pile of seemingly disconnected items, the order of which was easy for him to see but was incomprehensible to anyone else with the slightest aversion to clutter. Kaye did so much to save him from himself, forcing him every couple of weeks to make his pile comprehensible to "normal people." That meant filing. It was not his favorite subject.

Hand in hand, they ambled cozily up the slate walkway to the front porch. A newly installed handicap ramp became visible as they approached. A strategically located hedge blocked a direct view of the ramp. Workmen and local nursery landscapers had cleverly incorporated the hedge into the design of the porch and ramp, which sloped to the rear of the house and connected to the porte-cochere. The local men were proud of their craftsmanship and all too happy to be of service to the new young doctor in town and especially to his beautiful wife. After all, good Southern boys know exactly which side their bread is buttered on.

The couple steered themselves up the stairs to the double front door and its leaded glass windows. They peeked inside and saw Annie, the new office manager, scurrying around the front desk area putting things in their place. They could hear her barking orders at some hired workmen who were moving filing cabinets and furniture around.

"Should we say hi?" Keene offered.

"I think not," Kaye said. "We've got better things to do." She grinned suggestively.

They strolled arm in arm across the ramp side of the front porch, which displayed the rows of newly painted Windsor rocking chairs flanking the main entrance and hanging baskets of seasonal flowers along the Victorian-style porch rail. They followed the curve of the porch around and under the overhang of the porte-cochere to a high picket fence abutting the side and rear of the mansion. The picket gate was suspended and latched in place by black antique hardware hinges and lock. An arched trellis framed the gate and showcased a crimson explosion of Confederate Roses.

Inside the gate, a slate path ran straight back to another path, describing a perpendicular intersection ten feet or so from the gate. This path ran to the right at the front edge of a spacious courtyard to the porch at the rear of the mansion. To the left, the path stretched some twenty feet to another porch at the side of a large carriage house. That porch showcased a gabled roof that mimicked the architecture of the carriage house above it and the grand gables of the mansion. Along a stretch of this path, the shady sheltering arms of a wisteria-clothed arched trellis pointed the way between the new home and the new office of Daniel Keene, MD, and his bride.

"By the way ... those two hours I gave you to stop what you were doing starts now." She slipped off her running shoes and draped them on the artfully and practically placed hook inside the door. His shoes were soon draped intimately beside hers. "Don't wake up the puppy or we'll have company in the bed."

He pursued her up the stairs.

# HALO (CLASSIFIED)

The lights inside the C-130 cast an eerie green glow about the cargo compartment, complementing the green LEDs affixed to twelve helmets and jumpsuits. The engines droned.

"Ten thousand feet. Breathe deep, ladies. I mean all y'all, not you, Master Sergeant." The speaker was a tall, lanky fellow with slumped shoulders. He wasn't physically impressive, but he commanded the respect of the jumpmaster and the twelve combat-ready Force Recon personnel who were hooked up to the oxygen supply.

The sergeant chuckled. She knew their lives and well-being depended upon this yokel who, despite his redneck demeanor, was a highly trained PT (physiological technician) whose sole job was the health, safety, and operational readiness of the men (and woman) who were arrayed in formation along the jump seats.

"Okay, now," the jumpmaster interjected. "Headed for altitude. You heard PT. Breathe deep. Nobody gets the bends tonight."

The C-130 nosed up into a steep climb. The sergeant checked her gear for the hundredth time as they climbed, a habit cultivated over the years. "Can never be too careful," she thought.

"Drop zone coming up," barked the jumpmaster. "Switch out to O2 tanks." The marines disconnected from the oxygen supply on the fuselage and hooked up to the tanks they carried. Their helmets and face shields were firmly in place.

"Nobody leaves this flyin' junk heap with an O2 sat below ninety-two percent, so hook em' up good or you're spending the night with ME." The PT lingered over the threat with his Southern drawl just for effect.

The sergeant squirmed a little in the new gear they had been issued just for this mission. Underneath the combat gear was a new generation of dry suit. It was insulated, watertight, and hermetically sealed. It had to be.

"Okay, girls ... not you, Master Sergeant," the PT said again. "Button up those golden cufflinks. It's pushing minus thirty degrees out there and you're going into some major cold water on the other end. It is the North freaking Sea after all. You show some skin and you lose the use of your hand. Or lose the hand."

"Any final words before we go off intercom and get quiet as little mousies? Hmmm?"

"Yeah, I got something to say ..." It was one of the jumpers. "How does it feel, Top? Your last smash and grab party?" A general chuckle arose along with a couple of "Semper Fi" calls from the assembly as they waddled in two groups toward the opening cargo door.

"Another day at the office, Jackie-boy ... Gimme a gold watch tomorrow. Now shut up ... it's time to go quiet."

Two black pallets slid into the void, their green LEDs affixed and blinking softly as they disappeared in the darkness. Six Marines in a formation like a football huddle shuffled crabwalk-style in unison and followed the packages. The master sergeant and her group were immediately behind.

As she fell, the sergeant spread her arms and legs to stabilize the descent, keeping her eyes on her comrades. It was important to keep in contact and hit the water close enough to each other to assemble for action and get on board the Zodiacs that were preceding them into the frigid Arctic water. Despite the warm encasing wrap that she wore, the cold was still palpable as the 120-mph descent buffeted her body. She breathed in a controlled fashion, keeping her heart rate under control. "Old hat," she thought.

Suddenly, a jolt of panic hit her. "How could this be?" It was an uncharacteristic feeling. "I've been shot at (and hit). I've been tortured. I've been blown up. I'm still here, aren't I?

"Are there sharks in the North Sea?" Her mind was filled with the picture of the Jaws shark awaiting her landing with its gaping maw wide open, along with rows of razor-sharp teeth, waiting to sever her body in half and swallow the pieces. Try as she might, the vision would not depart.

Her controlled breathing disintegrated into hyperventilation.

Training still prevailed, however. The altimeter now read 3,500 feet. She opened the glide chute, which responded with a vigorous jolt. She worked hard to focus on the guys around her and steered her chute toward the packages on the ocean's surface. The Zodiacs were deployed and waiting.

That shark was also still waiting.

She hit the water and quickly detached her chute. She had nearly passed out from the over breathing. The landing and no shark in view brought her back to the moment. But she felt a wet warmth rising inside her suit from the region below her waist.

# UNREPORTABLE EVENT

"Oh, Lord," she exclaimed silently, "I've pissed myself." She stroked methodically and rhythmically through the water toward the blinking LEDs of the Zodiacs, surrounded by the company of a few good men.

A couple of clicks away, a trawler lay still, silhouetted against the dim horizon, the lights of the bridge and cabins casting a soft golden reflection upon the mirror of the sea. Such a glassy North Sea was virtually non-existent but yet here it was. It would make their access and egress much easier. This was their objective: "supposedly" a Norwegian fishing trawler. It was actually a Russian electronic intelligence-gathering vessel. Now its engines had failed, and it sat helpless. It was waiting for relief from the Russian warship that had been dispatched to come to its aid. The USA had other ideas.

The mission: get to that ship first and initiate a "VBSS," Force Recon style (Visit, Board, Search, and Seizure). The plan: get on, get the goods, get out, get to the fast attack, and disappear before the Russians got there. Simple.

"Okay, gonna get this done," the sergeant mused to herself.

The Zodiacs hummed through the darkness toward the becalmed trawler. They parted ways, one heading to the stern port side and the other the starboard. Silently they pressed their tiny vessels close beside the stricken ship. Small launchers appeared in the hands of the marines, and with a muffled *poof,* grappling hooks attached to ladders catapulted over the gunwales. The predators ascended quickly, grimly.

Fanning out in pairs, they swept forward from their position at the stern. Their presence was only betrayed by intermittent suppressed flashes accompanied by muffled *pffft* sounds and the thuds of Russian crew members flopping lifelessly to the deck.

The deck, bridge, crew quarters, mess hall, engine room, and work rooms were quickly neutralized. The sergeant and her team descended the ladder into the heart of the ship, breeched the comm room door with the help of small, shaped charges supplied by her teammates. The room was deserted, but the servers and electronic equipment hummed busily.

One marine spoke up. "Here's the server, Top." He reached out to turn the box so the ports would be accessible to a variety of plug-in drives that the sergeant and her data team had brought.

"Stop right there, Corporal!" the sergeant barked ferociously. "Jackie-boy, explain."

"See those wires there, buddy? It's not a server. It's a bomb."

"Shit! Sorry, Top."

"Got to find the real comm server. Fan out and look around."

Ten minutes later they were no closer to finding what they were looking for.

"Sarge, it's not here."

"Got to be ... No other place has the input this room has. Check that broom closet."

"Did that already, Sarge."

"Really?"

Just then the comms crackled. "Gotta move it, Sarge; intel says there's a Gorshkov Class Frigate over the horizon; got Kalibrs and Oniks and Redut on board. Nasty shit. And really fast movers. Don't care if that frigate is two hundred miles away. They can blow this bucket out of the water in seconds if they suspect we're here."

"Kick the back wall of that broom closet, Corporal. It looks kinda shallow for that space."

# UNREPORTABLE EVENT

The corporal obeyed, and true to her instincts, the back panel crumbled, revealing a rack of servers neatly stacked behind.

"Plug in the drives so we can get out of here."

In special ops terms, the download took an eternity. The comms crackled again. "Gotta go, Sarge ... like yesterday... SATCOM indicates missile launch!" The voice on the other end had raised at least an octave or two. "They don't want nothin' or no one gettin' outta here."

They snatched the drives and dashed for the ladder and up to the deck. The sergeant thought she saw a flash on the eastern horizon.

"No time to climb down, fellas. Jump." She knew about subsonic and hypersonic cruise missiles. "If it was anything other than a Kalibr, we'd already be toast." She hurled herself over the side, plunged the ten or fifteen feet into the frigid sea, and grabbed the handle on the side of the raft. No time to clamber over the rail. "Go, go, go, go, go ... GO!"

The Zodiac sped away with several team members hunkered within and three electronics team members clinging on the outside to the black gunwales. Pale green LED lights beyond the bow revealed the position of the other members of the team in the other Zodiac in rapid retreat, and a click further on, another pale green light signaled the position of their exfil, a US fast attack boat.

Suddenly, to the stern of the little Zodiacs, the Russian intelligence ship, sea and sky erupted into a Vesuvius of white, red, and green pyrotechnics. A cruise missile had struck home. A deafening concussion wave of sound and pressure swept over the trailing boat and its occupants, compressing their heads, ears, and chests like a vise. The trailing Zodiac to which the sergeant clung was tossed violently into the air, catapulting its occupants into the dark waters.

For a millisecond the sergeant remembered the pain of other explosions, then all went dark.

✲✲✲

"You okay, Top?"

"I been hurt worse." She grinned darkly as the cobwebs left her aching brain. "The drives ... everybody else, okay?"

"Oh, yeah, Sarge. Mission accomplished."

She sighed and lay back on the gurney wedged into the only space that would accommodate it on the submarine. Her guys had dragged her sorry ass across a half mile of freezing dark water and transported her below. She was out of her combat gear, but the dry suit (still a "wet" suit underneath) remained on her body. She looked down and did a quiet sitrep on herself.

"Oh, hell. I got some 'splainin' to do. Well, guess I have an excuse now. Nobody needs to know about the damn shark."

# DANNY, PART 1 (15 A.D.)

"But Mom, Dad, the bird was dead," a fifteen-year-old Danny protested from the back seat as they rode home from the Wednesday night prayer meeting.

"I know you'll always think so, dear," his mother said calmly.

"But don't you feel it when we're praying for somebody? I mean, this energy that flows from the top of your head to the back of your neck and down your arms when you touch somebody and pray for them?"

"You know, Danny, that's called an 'autonomic reflex' or 'automatic physical reflex' in the body when your emotions are at a high pitch." It was his dad who had spoken up. He was a certified anesthesia technician and had a decidedly physiological approach to all things emotional.

His mother wasn't much help either. She also was a science major, a biology teacher, and was strictly interested in the anatomy and physiology of things. "But don't let what I'm saying stop you from rubbing my shoulders. I swear, sometimes I do think you have magic hands."

"I second that, son," his father said. "If I believed in magic, I'd say you have magic hands, too. Mind giving my neck a little rub now?"

Nine years earlier when Danny was just six years old, a strange and terrifying event occurred in Danny's life on one of their frequent trips to their mountain cabin that he couldn't forget.

Their little cabin was nestled in a mountain valley with a stream running through the middle of it. The best part of the stream was a small waterfall that wrapped the cabin in a tranquil blanket of sound that soothed them all to sleep at night when the windows were open.

Their neighbor's cow pasture backed up to their property. Danny liked Mr. Chambers. He was affable and warm. He often let Danny ride with him on his tractor as he transported bales of feed to the galvanized metal stations around the pasture. He wore overalls that smelled of hay and sweat. Danny loved to ride with him as he fed the cattle. He loved the stories that Mr. Chambers told.

There was an old historic grain mill on the banks of the larger river into which Mr. Chambers' and the Keenes' stream flowed. The farmer would tell tales of Civil War conspiracies and gun-running, of moonshiners and their battles for territory. Some of these tales were taller than others but they contained enough historical truth to bring them to life for little Danny. Unfortunately, according to Mr. Chambers, the rum-running of the previous century had given way in modern days to drug-running. The old mill that had been the center of so much illegal activity in the past now housed a quaint pottery and mountain arts consignment shop. It was a popular tourist destination.

The cattle munched happily around the edges of the split rail and hog wire fence that enclosed the pasture. At the point where this fence reached the stream, stout lengths of heavy-gauge barbed wire traversed the flow, forming a barrier that the cows could not cross. Thus, they could not travel upstream onto the Keene's property. This wire fence connected to another fence on the opposite bank, which enclosed another pasture belonging to Mr. Chambers. Large granite rocks formed ramps on either side of the stream and the submerged path across it. This path allowed access and egress from one pasture to another across the flow. Cows would cross over here, muddying the waters downstream with their passage. There was a small veggie garden on the cabin side of the fence that featured tomatoes, cucumbers, squash, zucchini, and various melons, along with a couple rows of okra. Little Danny loved the planting and the picking, but not so much the weeding.

Just below the cow crossing, the little river sent off a side branch that meandered lazily out into the pasture before winding its way back to rejoin with the main flow. It had been carved out decades before by torrential rains and flash flooding. The result was that it created a one-acre island that housed a copse of poplars, oaks, hickories, and pines. In the center of this little wood was a small clearing where previous folks had created a fire pit. This pit was surrounded by two circles of large, smooth stones. The smaller stones (perhaps fifty of them, each about ten inches in diameter) marked the edge of the pit itself. In a larger circle around the pit and stones there sat about a half-dozen larger stones as big as ottomans, along with an equal number of short sections of wide tree trunks turned on end.

Danny would occasionally scale the pasture fence and visit the island clearing. He would sit on one of the tree trunk sections which, set on its end, was a perfect low stool to enjoy the firepit. He frequently took PB&J or bologna sandwiches that his mom made and spent the sunny afternoon days picnicking and listening to the mountain breeze in the treetops or watching the crows, buzzards, and occasional hawks circling against the blue sky above the trees.

To access the island, Danny made use of a fallen poplar whose roots had been undermined by high water, which had caused it to topple in a high wind. Half of the tree's roots formed a muddy, tangled, vertical and semicircular wall. The lower half remained buried and fixed on the edge of the island, thus keeping the tree alive. The tree created a foot bridge across which Danny would walk, tightrope fashion. He could very well have hopscotched across the large rocks that had been placed in the stream as a footpath, but that wasn't much of a challenge. There was also a dead pine next to the poplar that hadn't fared too well after its fall; the pine's root system was not enough to sustain it in a horizontal position. It had also served as a bridge for little Danny from time to time when he wanted an extra challenge. He had to travel cautiously across the pasture so as not to arouse the ire of the bull that frequently roamed about. It was all part of the magic of the mountain cabin.

Off the back of the cabin, a formerly screened-in porch extended toward the little river. Danny's father had replaced the screens with plexiglass. A deck wrapped itself around the porch. This deck extended on stilts out over the stream just above the waterfall. It was a magical place. Danny would sit for hours on the deck and drop his fishing line into the stream, catching an occasional trout. Many a lazy day were spent out there, fishing and watching the cows.

Unfortunately, large plexiglass windows and birds don't get along very well. Frequently when they were sitting in that sunroom, there would be a small vibrating thud as a bird, thinking it was flying into empty space, flew straight into the glass. Danny would watch in horror as the seemingly lifeless bird would lie motionless on the deck. Then he would rejoice as the bird twitched and shuddered back to life, shook its head, flapped its wings, and fluttered away.

But one day a bright red cardinal crashed into the glass window. It fell lifeless to the deck and didn't move. Danny waited expectantly. It still didn't move. He watched it for an hour. Nothing. He cried. Suddenly an overwhelming pain and compassion swept over him. He crept slowly and cautiously out of the porch door and approached the lifeless red bird. There was no breath, no movement.

He picked up the dead bird and cradled it gently in his hands. The bird's head flopped to one side. It appeared that its little neck was broken. But as he held the creature tenderly, he felt a warmth come over him. It started at the nape of his neck and spread across his shoulders, sending tingles down his arms. He felt his hands becoming hotter. Suddenly, with a shiver and a flap, the red bird's neck straightened and its wings spread and beat a rhythm against Danny's little palms. Then the bird sprang to its feet and fluttered away.

This moment was the early kindling on the fire that would later ignite in Dr. Daniel Keene, MD. From that point on, he knew he wanted to be a physician, a healer. He wanted to know everything that a person could know so he could bring life and health to other people. Boy Scout merit badges and the first aid courses he took in the following years were just not enough.

# UNREPORTABLE EVENT

"What if," he thought to himself, "I'm in a place one day where somebody goes down and someone cries out, 'Is there a doctor in the house?'" He would get a chance to experience that very thing years later. It even happened more than once, including in the middle of a big production of *Les Misérables* in the Fox Theatre in Atlanta.

✳✳✳

Danny loved those weekends at the cabin. He loved fishing. He loved following the trails to the top of the ridge. He would stop and listen to the sound of the stream at the bottom of the valley. He would crouch silently on the old logging trails and listen for the sound of animals (Foxes? Deer?) scampering just out of sight. Or was that a group of Confederate guerilla soldiers stealthily avoiding a Union patrol? His imagination thrived in the quiet of the Blue Ridge.

He especially loved climbing over the pasture fence, traversing the field, and tightrope walking across the downed poplar to the little island. As he followed the path to the center of the trees and sat for hours by the circle of stones in the little clearing, he imagined himself to be a backwoods pioneer on the frontier getting ready to uncover new and unexplored territory.

But one weekend was different. As Danny lay in his bunk bed in the loft of the cabin, drifting off to the sound of the waterfall, another sound reached his ear: it was a rhythmic, musical, chanting sound. Danny slid out from under the covers and edged over to the window that looked out upon the fence, the pasture, and the edge of the island.

A drum beat and an accompanying chant emanated from the island. Danny saw distinctly through the dense trees that a campfire was blazing in the small clearing at the center of the island. He couldn't make out anything else. He assumed some friends or family of Mr. Chambers were having a party and a campfire. It was a full two weeks later on their next trip that Danny detected something seriously amiss.

On that Friday, Danny and his family arrived at the cabin for the weekend. As usual, he made a beeline for the back porch, grabbing a fishing pole along the way. As he stepped out on the porch over the trout pool above the falls, eagerly snatching a wriggling worm to bait his hook, a foul odor invaded his nostrils.

"Yuuuckk!" he shouted. "Mom, Dad, something smells really bad out here!"

A pungent and rancid scent of something dead was wafting off the pasture. The cows munched away obliviously, except for one that sat away from the others at the edge of the little side stream.

"I think that's a momma cow," observed his mother. "Maybe something is down there by the stream."

"I'll check it out, Mom."

"Be careful, Danny."

Danny scurried down the porch steps and trotted across the grass, skirting the edge of the vegetable garden. He scaled the split rail fence quickly, and, keeping an eye out for the bull, traversed the edge of the pasture, making his way to the horizontal poplar tree. He quickly scampered across and followed the stench to the junction of the side branch and the main streams where the momma cow was keeping vigil.

He worked his way along the familiar path to the clearing at the center of the wood. The firepit showed signs of recent activity. As he approached the pit, he was puzzled to see that the stones closest to the pit, which had formerly been arranged in a circle, were now set in a five-pointed star pattern. He didn't know what that meant. He examined the pieces of charred debris in the pit. The campfire bore the same scent that it had on many other occasions when Mr. Chambers' hired hands or family had barbecues on that spot.

Danny looked around to see if anything else had changed. He saw an area at the periphery of the clearing where the underbrush of small saplings and scrub pine seedlings looked disturbed and a bit pressed down. Pretending to be a pioneer tracker, he followed the trail away from the circle and down toward the bank of the main stream. The rotten odor grew more intense as he neared the little river.

There, he saw it. Hidden in the brush and the tangle of blackberries that framed the stream junction was the decaying carcass of a calf. The stench brought tears to little Danny's eyes.

"Mom, there's a dead calf over here," he shouted, all the while suppressing the heaving, nauseous sensation that ascended from his gut. He got a little closer to the carcass and saw things that disturbed him: First, he saw that the head of the little calf was almost completely severed and its eyes were missing, gouged out. Second, the whole chest and abdomen of the little beast was sliced open. It appeared that nothing was left inside. A fearful uneasiness rose inside him that surpassed the revulsion of the gruesome sight before him.

With panic rising uncontrollably in his mind, Danny ran quickly back up the way he had come. The fear that permeated his body duplicated a sensation he had felt on many occasions in his own home; he always hated coming up the basement stairs at night. He had to turn off that basement light before running up. The pitch darkness at the foot of the stairs as he fled upward always threatened to reach out and drag him back into the abyss. Certainly, some foul, dark beast lurked below, just waiting for an opportunity to grab him before he could escape into the light. He could never suppress that thought in his little boy imagination. What he felt now as he ran from the bank of the stream was far worse.

He ran breathlessly across the island through the clearing to cross the fallen poplar tree and return to his mother, who waited at the back porch steps. As he hurriedly traversed the clearing, he glanced again at the star-shaped pattern of stones that previously had formed a circle around the firepit. But Danny was too spooked to stop and investigate any further.

"I wonder why Mr. Chambers hasn't gotten that poor thing out of there?" his mom enquired.

It turned out Mr. Chambers had been gone for a couple of weeks and had only just returned and discovered the unfortunate animal.

"Yeah, Miz Keene," he said as he leaned over the fence rail to inform them of his situation. "My hired help that was watching the place for me said they didn't know what to do. None of them knew anything about who might have done this. Sorry for the smell.

"Looks like whoever did this meant to drag that calf to the river in hopes it would float away downstream. But they got tangled in the blackberries and left it there. My guys didn't know what to do with the animal when they found it. There used to be a rendering place in the next county a few miles away, but they're closed now. And anyway, by the time they found him, that poor fella was too far gone to be of any use. So, I gotta bury him. The law says it has to be two hundred feet from the stream, so he'll be buried out in the middle of that pasture somewhere. Gotta get that little thing out quick before he fouls the river. They're setting up the front loader on my backhoe as we speak. The weird thing is that it's so torn up. Somebody was messing with that calf. I'm going to have to check that out."

Danny sat on the fence and watched the proceedings over the course of the afternoon. Mr. Chambers drove the tractor, with the backhoe on one end and a front loader on the other, down the cattle path that paralleled the wire fence across the stream. He steered it down the shallow rapids up to the junction with the small brook.

Plunging the front loader into the blackberries, he skillfully cleared away the underbrush. Then he deftly scooped the carcass into the bucket. The odor became even more unbearable since the calf's body had been partially dismembered. Danny retreated from the fence and fled to the glassed-in porch. Mr. Chambers had already dug a deep hole out in the pasture with the backhoe attachment.

His hired help sawed off the dead pine that traversed the stream and dragged it across the field. Then, after applying a chainsaw to the pine, they split it into dozens of resinous logs that they arranged in the bottom of the six-foot-deep grave. They dumped the carcass in and soon a brilliant orange blaze wrapped in pitch black smoke from the pine resin leapt from the hole, swirling upward in a furious whirlwind. Most of the smoke floated with the gentle wind blowing down the pasture, downstream like the little river, away from the cabin.

But something strange happened. While most of the smoke rode on the prevailing wind, which carried the mixed scent of pine resin, charred wood, and roasting rotted flesh away from the cabin, a single inky black whirlwind defied the breeze and pursued a contrary course, as if guided by an unseen hand, toward the cabin, enveloping it in a foul fog. The young hired men stood around, tending the conflagration.

No one seemed to notice the anomalous whirling black plume except for Danny.

It was more than the little boy could take. The acrid, rotting smoke stung his eyes and generally made him feel miserable. Frankly, it was downright *scary* to him. He retreated into the house and ran straight to the shower to wash off the awful stench.

The windows stayed closed that night. They would enjoy no soothing sounds from the waterfall as long as smoke rose from that pit.

"Mommy, can we go home tomorrow?" Danny asked later that evening. "It just smells so bad and … and I'm scared."

For weeks afterward, Danny couldn't shake that smell, real or imagined, that invaded his nostrils, unbidden, unwelcome, disturbing, and evil.

"Mommy, Daddy, can we not go back up there for a while?"

# DANNY, PART 2 (6-18 A.D.)

They did take a short break from excursions to the cabin. But, as always, time heals memories and they returned to their semi-monthly trips to the mountains. Danny's father, needing the break from life in the city and the hospital, craved the quiet and savored the never-ending maintenance and handyman tasks that presented themselves. He enlisted Danny's young hands to assist him. For the little boy, the memory of that terrifying weekend faded. He resumed his excursions across the pasture, to the island, and up the mountain ridge to play pioneer and explorer.

The vigorous walks he took alone (and sometimes with his dad) led to an exceptionally strong pair of legs that Danny put to good use on hikes as a Boy Scout and, when he entered high school, as a rising star on the cross country team. This led to an athletic scholarship at a prominent southern university, where he plunged into a strong science curriculum to prepare himself for medical school. He still wanted to be a healer. The memory of that dead bird never faded.

He continued to have recurrent dreams: tornado dreams. They started shortly after the incident at the cabin and continued from time to time over the years. The theme was nearly always the same: He might be watching from a distance in fearful curiosity as the multiple twisters of various sizes danced along the horizon. He might be on a country road as he drove along in a car. Sometimes he would be in his house and the tornado would be raging outside, invisible yet violently palpable. He was always strangely attracted and inquisitive, always trying to get closer to the whirlwinds but never really able to do so. But one thing was for sure; though he was unable to get closer to the tornadoes in his dreams, over time they were getting closer to him. He wondered what this meant.

Through his teens, he often participated in prayer meetings either at his church or with a high school fellowship group that assembled at a local residence. He continued to experience the surging warmth in his arms and hands when praying for others and laying hands on them. Being the inquisitive sort, he harbored questions about what was actually happening. He read books about spiritual healing; not all were from a Christian perspective. He was intrigued by the New Age bookstores and often wondered to himself and to his close friends, "Why do all these pagans seem to have cornered the market on healing energy and 'miracle cures'?" About the most of an answer he ever got was a shrug of the shoulders.

Once enrolled in his university, he took an introductory philosophy course as an elective alongside his heavy basic science curriculum. School was great; cross country even better. He'd made the All-Conference team and the dean's list.

At the close of the first term, Danny crawled into his bunk after his last final. He had finished off the term with straight As, gone out for a celebratory run, partied with his buddies, then sunk into his bed late. He was planning to drive home early the next morning to spend the Christmas break with his family and friends. He fell asleep quickly in joyful anticipation of the vacation to come.

He awoke in the pitch darkness with the sound of crashing and crackling all around him and the feeling of being buffeted and rocked by a violent wind. "The dorm is on fire?" he wondered. "Is it a real tornado?"

He tried to throw off the covers and get up and out, but he couldn't move. It was just like the time when, clowning around during a sleepover with rowdy friends as a ten-year-old, he had been trapped headfirst in a sleeping bag. It was a horrible experience. They had laughed hysterically but he had been in a claustrophobic panic. The more he screamed the more they laughed.

This was far worse. The whirling blackness continued to engulf him as he struggled to breathe, to cry out for help, to escape. He was caught in a vortex of sound like that of a thousand freight trains.

"Where are my suitemates?" He tried to call for help but no sound escaped his lips. The stench of burning, rotting flesh permeated his nostrils. He was a little boy again, looking out over the mountain pasture at the black smoke that had swept over him like a tide, filling his soul with dread and the sensation of pervasive evil.

He finally woke up and slapped himself over and over just to be certain. All was quiet. His dorm room, no longer pitch black, was illuminated by the small night light in the corner socket. Nothing had changed. The sense of dread persisted. Danny rolled over and pulled the covers over his head as if to shut out the horror that had just invaded his room and his sleep. He had control over these covers; he wasn't stuck like he'd been in that sleeping bag. "Just a nightmare, another tornado dream," he thought as he drifted back off into a fitful sleep for the remainder of the night.

The next morning, he was startled awake by the sound of his cellphone ringing.

"Hello?"

"Danny, are you coming home today?" It was his father.

By the tone in his voice, Danny knew something was seriously wrong.

"What is it, Dad?"

"It's your mom. Get home as quickly as you can, but drive safe."

The news when Danny got home was grim. There had been no sign of anything wrong until mere hours before he was planning to come home. In the weeks prior, Mrs. Keene had not suspected anything out of the ordinary. Yes, she had been experiencing some uncharacteristic headaches, but nothing more. But when these headaches accelerated, she went to the emergency department.

Blood tests, spinal tap, and other diagnostic procedures revealed nothing. But the MRI of the brain showed otherwise. His mother suffered from glioblastoma multiforme, the most aggressive form of brain tumor. Because it had arisen in a part of the central nervous system that did not control major motor or sensory functions, its presence had gone undetected until it had spread its tentacles broadly. Now there would be no effective treatment. She had only weeks, or even days, to live.

"Thank you for praying for me," his mom said weakly. "You don't need to worry about me. I know where I'm going."

These were among the last words that she said to him as he kept vigil by her bedside over the entire Christmas break.

She went home before school started again in the second term.

# AKHTAR (21 A.D.)

Johannes Akhtar was a superstar. He was the gifted grandson of Turkish immigrants who had found their way to Germany after WWII. He was smart. Supersmart. Educated. His parents had given him a German first name but had kept the surname. After a stellar performance at the Technical University of Munich, he was recruited into the pharmaceutical industry. There he rose swiftly through the ranks, and at a young age he was now in one of the highest positions in Big Pharma: chief of operations at Pelzer Pharm, an international powerhouse. The company derived its name from its humble beginnings as a small generic drug manufacturing plant in the small South Carolina town of Pelzer.

In his early adulthood as his career was skyrocketing, he had basked in the prestige, money, and other perks of the gilded life. His encyclopedic brain had enabled him to succeed at whatever he ventured, including investments and a multiplicity of business deals he exploited even as he served as COO. He was a rich playboy. He knew all the right people. He went to all the right places. Whether it was a celebratory event for some member of European royalty or a Formula One event, he was never seen without some supermodel on his arm. His was a Falstaffian existence.

But he was not happy. "There must be more than this," he lamented to himself as he gazed blankly over the Munich skyline from his luxurious apartment. It featured one of two Picassos that he owned. The other hung in his office.

"Johannes, my child," his mother implored one day. "You work too hard. You seem so distracted, so unhappy. You need to get away for a bit. Why don't you go see our family in Turkey? My sister and her husband would love to entertain you in Istanbul. Please, my son. Your life, so full of everything that the world can provide, is so empty. Please take this." She handed him a copy of the Koran. He tucked it into his pocket and promptly forgot about it. He humored his mother and stated he would probably visit the home country soon.

He returned immediately to the grind and glamor of his high-profile corporate and social life. Each night he would return to his luxury flat, either alone or in the company of some fabulously beautiful fashion model or European princess. But, one night, things changed.

He came home early to sink into bed, exhausted from the day's labor and libations. Without even shedding his clothes, he sprawled across the satin sheets and promptly fell into a deep sleep.

A sudden noise like that of distant thunder and the rending of tree trunks aroused him. The room was darker than usual. It seemed not to be taking up the ambient light from the Munich skyline as it usually did. An intense fragrance permeated his nostrils, a smoky, burning aroma, pungent but not unpleasant. Shaking the cobwebs from his brain, he momentarily forgot the uncharacteristic darkness and sought out the source of the odor.

Before long he traced the origin of the fragrance. It emanated from the Koran that he had carelessly tossed on his night table days before. He hadn't thought of it since. Now, however, he was transfixed by the book, not only because of the incense of sandalwood that flowed out of it, but also because of the curling plume of black smoke that rose from it, ascending toward the ceiling in swirling arcs and dissipating across the expensive millwork and recessed lighting overhead.

A sudden compulsion flooded over him, steering him to pick up the small volume from the table. A voice echoed in his ears. "I AM KREEEV-DAH!" it intoned in a mysterious, raspy way that carried strange trickling vibrations, as of spring water over rocks at the side of a mountain trail. He looked intently about the room, trying to discern where the sound came from. The voice had seemed to emanate from his own head. It spoke again. "All that you seek is here!" His eyes were drawn to the book he held in his hands and now opened expectantly.

Akhtar read: "In the name of Allah, the Compassionate and Merciful. Praise be to God, Lord of the worlds …" He read on: "Thee we worship and from Thee we seek help …"

The unveiling of a revelation began there in the semi-darkness. Could it possibly be that in all his affluent self-sufficiency, he was in dire need of help? As if to answer that unspoken thought, the whispered voice of this mysterious "Krivda" continued in his head and repeated, "Here is the help you seek!" He clutched the book to his breast and decided to make the journey to Istanbul, per his mother's wishes. A nagging compulsion now drove him to seek out a family he had never met for a reason he had yet to discern.

Upon his arrival in Istanbul, Johannes was greeted warmly by family members he had only heard of. He was surrounded with warmth and love and closeness. He had sweet communion with cousins, aunts, uncles, and a never-ending parade of friends of the family.

In Turkey he felt even more acutely the dark void at the center of the life he had been leading. Back in Germany, with frequent hops to Manhattan and a life full of every material and earthly thing his heart desired, he could never escape the inner nagging, an angst that cast a shadow on his soul. The emptiness had grown intolerable.

"Come. Sit here with us, *tatlim*." His aunt beckoned him to the chair next to her to share the feast. Freshly made hummus and a host of other delicacies created a culinary landscape across the hexagonal table at the side of the kitchen. A finer charcuterie spread he had rarely seen, even in the best restaurants in Munich and Manhattan.

"Thank you, my *teyze*," he replied softly, taking a seat beside her.

✯✯✯

It did not take long for Akhtar to shed himself of his daily European routine and to adapt to the flow of life in a devout Turkish Muslim home. He also shed his "cutter bespoke" Italian-cut suits for a simple kaftan as the loathing of everything in his spoiled, rich life continued to fester inside him. He envied the quiet devotion of this family; the peace they exuded was palpable as they responded to the daily call to prayer, reciting the Shahadah at its beginning and end. He began to join in. Here in the bosom of his kinsfolk, reading daily in his copy of the Koran that still carried the scent of sandalwood incense, he discovered the only thing that could fill the void of his aching materialistic heart.

The message now permeating his soul told him only complete devotion to Allah could bring the peace and meaning he so craved. Absolute obedience was all that Allah required. Here in the embrace of his family, his conversion and conviction became swift and severe, driven by a passion that exploded as a pyroclastic flow from the core of his Olympian spiritual energy and intellect. Day after day he responded to the call to worship, kneeling devoutly among his new spiritual brothers. He listened raptly to the words of the Imam, with whom he soon confided.

"I despise my former life," he hissed. "I hate the world in which I'm living. It is most evil. I believe this way must be destroyed along with everything that wars against Allah the Most Merciful. I wish I could bring it all down. Imam, can I tell you this? I have resolved to publicly renounce my old life! I have decided to cast aside all worldly pleasures, the drinking, the women, material goods, and to walk away from the sins of the Kafir!"

"I sense that in you there is a better way to serve Allah," whispered the Imam. "Allah can use you best to strike a blow against the world of the Kafir. But to do this you must remain secret. Do not let them know. *Taqiyya!* It is the will of God. Let Allah and the Prophet—may his name be forever blessed—guide you in what you are destined to do. He has put you in a powerful position, my son. Use that."

Akhtar bowed solemnly to the Imam as he took his exit. Glancing back at the holy man, who was receiving other disciples, he could see distinctly a swirl of dark incense rising from the space around the kilim floor cushion upon which the man sat, and he could smell the aroma of sandalwood.

✡✡✡

Akhtar returned to his life in Europe. He donned his Saville Row attire once more and resumed his duties. In obedience to the Imam, he changed nothing on the outside that could give anyone a clue to his newfound faith.

A grand idea was incubating inside him; the best way to strike a powerful blow against the Kafir, he reasoned, was to utilize his position, which required him to commute regularly to Manhattan and to other places around the globe. He could exploit the resources afforded to him by his associations with dozens of influential people.

Johannes was, himself, in an ideal position to wreak havoc. He was in command of the development, supply chains and logistics, manufacturing, and distribution of many of the most widely used medicinal products on the planet. He pondered the "Tylenol Scare" of 1982 that had led to a US national mandate for sealed containers for all medicinal substances, both over-the-counter and prescription. Forty people had died from the cyanide-laced painkiller. He had plans for something bigger, much bigger.

Many of Akhtar's contacts dwelt on the shadowy side of international commerce, especially in Eastern Europe. With a discreet inquiry or two through former members of the Stasi, Johannes and Pelzer were now able to possess, via the black market, many new (or at least unconventional) pharmacological agents. Getting one of them reproduced and distributed was just a matter of making the right connections. For many months, he had been exploiting professors and researchers in several major American medical schools. They were helping him shortcut the costly research and development process, performing off-the-books, investigations in their clinics and allowing Pelzer to observe the initial effects of experiments under the watchful eyes of experts and away from the eyes of federal investigators.

✯✯✯

"There's a courier here for you, sir." The secretary spoke across Akhtar's massive chrome and glass desk.

"Show him in."

The young man in a leather motorcycle jumpsuit strode across the room, helmet under one arm and zippered box under the other.

"Set it here ..." Akhtar gestured casually to the empty space in front of him, trying his best to convey an air of nonchalance. The courier complied and took a backward step, remaining at semi-attention.

Akhtar opened the box and carefully extracted a nondescript rectangular plastic container with snap closures on the corners and security seal tape across the top. Suppressing the trembling in his hands as he produced a small box-cutter blade, he sliced the tape, raised the corner snaps, and lifted the lid. The courier was dismissed.

Now Akhtar was ready to get on with the first phase of his plan. He would use his covert American investigators to do some initial testing. Then he would manufacture large quantities of the potion that lay before him, the innocent-appearing medicinal vials in Styrofoam rows like so many soldiers in formation, waiting to be deployed. Years of preparation along his rise through the ranks of the international pharmaceutical industry had brought him to this point.

Akhtar hadn't acquired a personal fortune just from his salary with Pelzer Pharma and his savvy investing. As he had worked his way up the corporate ladder through pharma supply and logistics, he had discovered a profitable sideline. Chinese manufacturers of every conceivable item around the world were always lining up to offer cheaper production of these goods to Western companies looking to sell things at a lower price.

With the support and sanction of the Chinese Communist Party, these manufacturing moguls would line up and compete with each other. They offered manufacturing contracts to eager entrepreneurs from around the globe, many of whom had just a prototype and an idea. If the Chinese supplier could get a contract for a minimum of a container load of a certain item—whether it be a new line of bedroom slippers, or orthopedic foot fracture shoes, or kitchen widgets—they would take the contract. Imagine their eagerness to manufacture medicine bottles, delivery devices, and other things ancillary to the business of a giant like Pelzer. Akhtar was able to finesse these deals with Chinese businessmen. He was also inclined to take the offers from those who provided him a little personal incentive through numbered Swiss bank accounts.

The next phase of his plan could not, however, take place under the corporate umbrella. He would have to handle the arrangements personally and verbally, not via emails, cellphones, and company communications.

He now had the ideal cover for personal communication. Akhtar would continue to "visit family" many times in Turkey. He journeyed eastward under the premise of exploring the land of his heritage. But he went further east and quietly slipped over the border. He travelled from Kapikoy in Turkey to Razi in Iran in order to meet his Chinese contacts in Tabriz. He was following the "New Silk Road," also known as the Belt and Road Initiative, part of the strategic global plans of the Chinese Communist Party. He walked across the floral tiles of the Blue Mosque, backpack slung from his kaftan-clad shoulders. He then ambled through the marketplace, weaving his way among the women all dressed in niqabs in observance of their faith.

It was easy to meet his Chinese allies there. They were, after all, in lockstep with the rulers of Iran, who allowed such transactions to flow smoothly as long as they were assured the ultimate goal of such meetings was the destruction of the "Great Satan." The Chinese emissaries with whom he met represented chemical manufacturing companies who could produce anything in large quantities. China was good at that, since it could always find someone who could rip off products and disguise them in authentic-looking packaging. Packaging and blueprints for US products were easy to obtain, courtesy of the security protocols that Chinese students and technical specialists embedded in the US had stolen in obedience to or in fear of the Chinese Communist Party authorities. China could smuggle almost anything into the States (and other countries) either illegally via the cartels of Mexico or through the legal importation process with help from high places. The country had done such a good job already, especially with weapons and fentanyl.

✯✯✯

Finally, after years of preparation, Akhtar's opportunity had arrived. Demonstrating the ability to execute the first phase of his plan meant he could carry out the next phase. This would bring the Infidel to his knees! The first phase was merely injecting a little poison into the system, a fine experiment for certain. It was just to be his little demonstration project to show it could be done. He was already using his allies at one American medical school to test it.

Striking a killing blow to the Great Satan of the West was a big project. That was the ultimate goal, and he was fervently developing the means. It was one thing to drip out a hallucinogen through the sampling process. He had already carefully planted his people inside the FDA to keep track of any "adverse event" reports that might start trickling in. He had instructed his insiders to make sure these reports would be "spiked." Furthermore, he was making sure the locales where these samples were distributed would be widely dispersed so as not to arouse suspicion.

He would soon be poised to get something else into the pharma supply chain, something awesome, wonderful, and catastrophic. He was planning to develop the means to deliver a death blow to the West courtesy of his Chinese allies. He sang praises to Allah Most High at the ease with which things had come together so far. He knew it was the will of Allah that caused his plans to move along so quickly and smoothly.

He was planning a visit to Brussels in the near future. He would certainly make good use of infidels who didn't understand the real purpose of what he was doing, but whose goal was the same as his.

# DANNY, PART 3 (23 A.D.)

Daniel took a seat on the grassy lawn of the County Mental Health Center. Today he was participating in a rotation in the Emory University School of Medicine psychiatric department. The Mental Health Center was where some of the most troubled, psychotic—and therefore "interesting"—patients were housed. Students were encouraged to take notes and explore the interviewee's thought processes, family history, patient history and experience, drug use, and so on. High on the list of topics were the genetic predisposition of the patient, the relationship of past trauma to their current mental state, and above all else to explore the possible medical or pharmaceutical interventions that might help.

On this occasion, the attending psychiatrists and psych nurses chose certain patients that they deemed safe to interview and paired them up with medical students for one-on-one sessions. The name of the patient to be interviewed was Alex. He had been incarcerated in the facility after he had been picked up by the local authorities. He had been running naked and wild in the woods, sacrificing animals around a raging bonfire.

# UNREPORTABLE EVENT

Keene had previous experience with a schizophrenic cousin. Conversations with him always seemed to gravitate toward cosmic and theological issues. Curiously, his cousin's bizarre ideations made a certain kind of sense. Keene came to learn people with the purported diagnosis of schizophrenia had a strong tendency to think on the mystical and spiritual aspects of life. Alex was on a whole different plane.

Keene and Alex sat cross-legged on the turf facing each other. It was a sunny, breezy, and cool spring day. The low clouds scudded overhead in a hurried procession, alternately blocking and revealing the radiant sun, which was set against a vibrant and clear blue sky. The net result upon the grassy lawn that afternoon, much like dramatic stage lighting effects, was a rapidly alternating atmosphere of light and dark.

"I made it do that," said Alex, as the patch of sunlight they were in suddenly dimmed as a cloud passed over.

"What do you mean, Alex?"

"When I feel bad it gets dark, and when I feel good, light."

"So you're switching back from good to bad right now?"

"Sure, Doc."

Keene's mind wandered between the absurd notion Alex was controlling the weather and the connection between this and the other strange ideas Alex had been expressing. The majority of the time, Alex's recitations were perfectly normal; that is, he spoke coherently and articulately about his past, childhood abuse, the suicidal brother, the drug use, and more.

But as the session progressed, the monologue from this psych patient was becoming increasingly disjointed, full of religious references from every faith under the sun.

"Y'know, Doc," Alex said, "I'm really a Hindu. I am one with the Universe. Everything is one. Funny, ain't it, that we believe everything is one, but us Hindus have more gods and demigods than any other religion." He had a point.

Keene had been reading a book about spiritual warfare, about the multiplicity of gods and demons in many religions. He was curious about the influence of the spiritual realm upon this unusual guy. A sudden whim captured his thoughts. Could Alex be possessed? So, he blurted out, "I want to talk to ALEX."

What happened next was unsettling. Alex's breathing became raspy and hissing as he leaned forward toward the medical student. Keene was afraid he was about to be attacked. Instead, Alex said to him in the most sinister and mocking way, in a voice like that of falling water, "I've already been EXORCISED! And it didn't work."

Keene felt his eyes stinging, and the acrid odor of burning pine and rotten flesh permeated his senses. He felt himself drawn into a vision of that cow pasture seventeen years earlier, as well as the night he dreamed of the smoky tornado, just before receiving word of his mother's fatal prognosis. A vibratory sensation, like that of a coarse dental drill, penetrated his tailbone and ascended upward along his spine. All his hairs stood on end. He felt himself slipping into unconsciousness.

"Doc! Hey Doc!" Alex was shaking him. "You okay?"

Keene abruptly came to his senses. "Uh, I think I just had an allergy attack," he lied. "All this early spring pollen in the air and all. I'm fine."

Across from him, Alex looked perfectly normal once again. Keene, on the other hand, was shaken and he brought the interview to a close as quickly as he could.

This wasn't the only unsettling experience Keene had that summer between his first and second years of medical school. The other one was on rotation in the University Chronic Pain

Management Center. The two attending physicians who ran the center were quick to take Daniel under their wing. They said they saw in him great potential in their field, due to what they perceived was his insight and empathy toward the patients.

They taught him, among other things, how to do paraspinal ganglion block injections deep in the neck, adjacent to the cervical spine. They introduced him to the use of various drugs for the treatment of chronic pain. Many of these drugs had not yet been cleared by the FDA for the general public, but this was research, clinical trials. A major supplier and partner in the process was Pelzer Pharma. They were studying how one such drug, which didn't have a trade name yet but went by the label of PX 91, would affect a patient's perception of pain.

Each day Keene sat at his cubical in the pain clinic, charting the progress of a couple dozen or so patients to whom he had administered nerve blocks. He noted several had also been prescribed PX 91 as part of their protocol. What puzzled him was one by one, each of these patients dropped out of the program. He was unable to find out if they had gotten better or if something else had happened. When he inquired about the dropouts to the registrar in charge of the research, all he received was a vague and unsatisfying response: the patients had voluntarily quit the program. No other answer was forthcoming. He asked the attending physicians about it and received the same response.

Then one day, a little more than halfway into his rotation, he was leaving the clinic when he heard animated voices from one of the doctor's offices. All he could make out through the closed door was, "Crazy … seeing things … left his body!" Keene determined to find out what this was about, although he knew the direct approach would not work.

# KAYE (23 A.D.)

Keene had first seen her in the crowd at a Campus Christian Fellowship group at Emory, that prominent southern medical school in Atlanta where the undergraduates were all "pre-something" and headed for bigger things. The med students had all been Phi Beta Kappas as undergrads or were already master's degree recipients in biological or biochemical sciences.

She had been a nursing student.

Having been a cross country runner in college and knowing what being in world-class physical condition was, Keene had kept a routine of running in med school. And one day he spied her again as he jogged on a path through the gardens of the estate adjacent to the campus. He recognized her from behind. Her golden ponytail flashed back and forth with each elegant stride. He wasn't looking at the ponytail.

He made a point to pursue her. Literally. He was definitely enjoying the view while quietly chastising himself for the carnal thoughts that flooded his brain. After all, he had a core set of beliefs in the evangelical world ruling out any actions on his part that might violate his conscience. But the gardenias along the running path only reinforced the passion building in his body.

The chase was on, and, as often as he could, he would spot her lithe figure and join in the pursuit, happy to stay incognito, at least for a while.

"Are you stalking me?" She confronted him as he rounded a blind curve she had only recently turned.

Totally flummoxed, his face turning crimson, he froze, speechless.

"So just stop it! And right now!" She turned and started to jog away, but he caught the slightest sly smile that turned up one corner of her incredible mouth with those luscious lips. "Name's Kaye." She darted out of sight.

The pursuit turned into several coffee dates at the student center.

"So, you're a medical student, huh?" was her opening line over their first latte in the center.

"'Fraid so. Just started second year. You?"

"Nursing, first year. And the next obvious question is, what made you decide to become a doctor?"

"You ready for the eloquent answer or the corny answer?"

"Either."

"I just wanted to help people ... Boy Scout, you know?"

"Laconic. But eloquent enough."

"Laconic? Who uses words like that?"

"English major ... but always wanted to be a nurse. You?"

"Philosophy. Weird, huh? And I stuffed in enough science to meet the basic requirements and scored pretty well on the MCATs."

"Genius boy."

"Nope. Just really motivated."

"Why philosophy?"

"I guess it's just because I always had questions about the nature of, well, *everything*, from, shall we say, a *non-scientific* perspective?"

"Ooooo, that's heavy," she said mockingly.

"Not really. You see, my mom died halfway through my freshman year. She had an aggressive brain tumor that had grown and spread before it caused any symptoms. It really killed me."

Kaye's expression went from playful to somber.

"Even though we always went to church and believed in the power of prayer, I guess I just plunged into a really dark, skeptical space in my head. I had just had my first course in philosophy. So, I just kept going. But I did manage to stay with enough of the pre-med stuff to keep that door open. And here I am."

"I'm so sorry." After a brief but awkward silence, she said, "Um, where do you live?"

"Little Five Points."

Keene lived in a truly funky area of town that he described to others as an artsy-crafty haven for burnt-out hippies, avant-garde artists, other bohemian types, and sundry refugees from the sixties and seventies.

The local pub that he frequented when he could was unique. Instead of "call me for a good time" and other more pornographic scribbles, the graffiti in the bathroom stalls featured quotes from Descartes, or Thoreau, or Nietzsche, or Sartre. His favorite was from Emerson: "A foolish consistency is the hobgoblin of little minds." He took that one, especially, to heart. He also had a button on his white medical school jacket that read: "Minds are like parachutes. They only function when open."

# UNREPORTABLE EVENT

The area suited his predispositions immaculately, as he was a philosophy major and not a "pre-med." Every conceivable religion and esoteric group was amply represented at one time or another in his neighborhood: Scientology, Hare Krishna, Moonies, Bahá'í, an ashram for followers of a celebrity *swami*, the House of Wicca, and more, not to mention every variation of Christian and pseudo-Christian churches. These were all within a half-mile radius of each other. His favorite, however, was the First Existentialist Fellowship; a delicious oxymoron, he mused.

Whenever he could, he would strike up conversations with the various religious and cult members he would meet on the streets of Little Five. He was eager to glean insights and information from people whose religious world views were so at odds with the American Judeo-Christian mainstream. The Hare Krishnas, he soon observed, were not much fun to talk to because they were really more interested in reciting their mantra over and over in their minds and out loud and never really engaged in a decent exchange of ideas.

Being a philosophy major had been a bit of a handicap during the basic sciences years at Emory. He had been clearly underprepared for the heavy science curriculum and rather out of place in this medical school class full of science nerds. They were "gunners," every one of them. Other things had been more important to him, as the sudden death of his mom several years previously had triggered a deep questioning of his world view and all his theological presuppositions. He had delved deeply into the study of religion and philosophy, questioning everything. He knew he was a committed Christian, but in his heart, he had almost left the fold.

As he sat across the table from this cute nursing student, his mind wandered to the fragrance of those gardenias along the running trail. He knew they would always remind him of the running girl with the ponytail. In a moment of impulsive transparency, he confessed this to Kaye across the table.

"Did you know," he said, following up his confession, "that the memory center in the brain is right next to the smell center just above the right ear? I learned that in neuroanatomy. That's why the perfume industry is so big. And speaking of smell and memory, my mom used to wear this certain perfume. Every time I smell it somewhere, I kinda tear up."

Kaye's eyes misted a little. Keene picked up on that and broke the second awkward silence of the conversation.

"So, where do you live?"

"Oh, I live up in Buford with my mom. Most of the other students are staying in the nursing dormitory. I think they want to hang around the campus all the time because half of them just want to marry a doctor. But Mom's a widow and I'm the only one still at home. We don't live in the nice part where they're gentrifying all the new houses. Still kind of on the back streets. Dad died when I was ten, and mom's been working in the public-school library as an assistant ever since. We don't have much money."

"Why nursing?"

"Same as you, I guess. I just like taking care of people … Girl Scout." Another grin. "And I can see you like to scout girls, too!" Her grin broadened.

Daniel blushed. He thought to himself, "No, just you." But what he said was, "I ran cross country in college; can I help it if there's always some girl I'm catching up to on the trails? I caught you, didn't I? Well, I guess you caught me!"

Keene's unconventional reputation spread among his classmates and even among the faculty. When they all sat around on weekends drinking beer, his compatriots would egg him on as he would pontificate on the mysteries of the body, soul, and spirit.

"What are you doing in med school, Keene?" they taunted. "You need to be teaching philosophy!"

One of his professors on his Internal Medicine rotation even wrote on his evaluation: "Dr. Keene is becoming an excellent diagnostician. He has a bright future ahead of him, although his methods are more 'impressionistic' than they are 'systematic.'" True, he was constitutionally unable to practice medicine by the book.

✫✫✫

That night Keene drifted happily off to sleep, replaying the memory of his coffee date with the now irresistible Kaye. His window was open, and the sounds of the street wafted in with the cool fall breeze: an occasional car passing by, the animated conversations of friends and lovers strolling up the hill toward the Tavern at L'il Five, the distant celebratory cacophony of the Hare Krishnas' drums and tambourines on the next block echoing off the buildings, the pavement, the sidewalks, the playground tennis courts.

> *They stood on the seashore, toes buried in the sand, holding hands, fingers intertwined. The breeze propelled to the shore by the crashing waves blended with the celebratory cries of happy children behind them on the beach.*
>
> *The wind picked up suddenly, a breeze to a gale, overpowering the waves and the children. The spray stung their cheeks. "Let's go inside, Daniel."*
>
> *"No, wait a minute, Kaye. Look at the waterspouts!" A dozen or more whirling, spraying vortices danced across the horizon, marching*

*like soldiers in formation in a tactical advance toward the couple. A single larger spout separated from the others and progressed in a straight line toward them.*

"We need to run!" Kaye tugged urgently on his hand.

"No, wait." Daniel took several steps forward into the surf. The larger vortex surged closer and still closer. Instead of fear, an intense fascination overcame him, instead of terror, an overwhelming curiosity. He reached out his hand. The wall of spinning water came closer still ...

"Don't touch it!" she screamed. "Daniel, DANIEL!"

# GATEWAY (23 A.D.)

"I haven't told you what I did this past summer." Daniel sipped his latte and leaned forward a little. They were taking up where the last coffee date had ended.

"What?" Kaye asked, leaning forward.

"Hold onto your hat now. I did a six-week stint in the chronic pain clinic here at the school. Two very interesting docs run this program. They're both anesthesiologists. Dr. Bruno and Dr. Samin. Dr. Bruno is from Eastern Europe, Croatia, I think. Dr. Samin's original name was Samanta. He's from India. Don't know why he changed his name. They have a program for evaluating and treating chronic pain. But more interesting than that, they are really into some *mystical* stuff.

"Now, I told you I went to a pretty standard Methodist church as a little boy. Then I 'found Jesus' when I was about fourteen. I made a bigtime commitment, got hooked up with the remnants of the 'Jesus Movement.' I'd been looking for something deeper, you know what I mean?" Keene was a bit worried as he confessed this. "I was done with that humdrum God. I guess you could say I became somewhat of a 'holy roller.'

"I saw miracles everywhere, spiritual warfare, prophecy and all that. That's when I really got into 'the laying on of hands.' My mom and dad really didn't believe in all that, but they both admitted that I had 'the touch.'

"Now, here I am in medical school. Sometimes I feel a bit out of place, cause I'm still the philosopher that I became in college. I really want to understand things, y'know? Like, I mean, what explains the phenomenon of spontaneous, miraculous healing in patients? Nobody knows. Why do some patients, when they've had a breakthrough experience, like some kind of spiritual awakening, sometimes suddenly get well in the face of incurable disease, metastatic cancers, inoperable tumors? Or why do others, without any such experience, have the same thing happen to them while others are praying for them? Oh, and it's not exclusive to Christianity."

"I know that." Kaye responded tentatively, baffled and intrigued at Daniel's disclosures.

"So, what is the power of prayer and faith? I feel energy when I'm taking care of patients or when I was a kid and used to rub my mom's back. In high school I got involved with some Bible studies and prayer groups. Some of them were what you call 'charismatic.' I've been prayed over and have prayed over others, laid hands on people. What's that thrill, that power you feel in your body from the top of the head to the back of the neck and down the arms when you touch another person in prayer? Is it just an emotional, autonomic, biochemical response like my mom and dad used to say? Ha! In the philosophy of science, we call that the reductionist approach. It's the way the Western scientific and academic world looks at everything. But surely something else is at play here,"

"All right, Keene, you're freaking me out here. You're talking to a philosophical materialist."

"Where did you learn that term, English major?"

"Philosophy 101. Prerequisite. Hated it."

"Well, back to these pain clinic guys." Keene was eager to get it all out there. "They've mixed some very interesting concepts from Eastern and Western medicine. What was really cool is they brought in this guest speaker, a Japanese electrophysiologist. He's a PhD but also a Shinto priest, of all things. He did a demonstration in the lecture hall of the pain clinic that just blew my mind.

"It seems during his research years ago he had gotten very stressed and developed some gastric ulcers. Same time he developed rashes on both of his shins that followed the stomach meridian of acupuncture. So, he got the idea to try to figure out a way to detect and map these meridians, the energy pathways through the body. And he did.

"This he did by placing electrodes on the fingertips of his subjects, applying electrical impulses, and measuring where these impulses showed up along each patient's skin and body surface. He was able to detect very distinct pathways that corresponded exactly to the traditional acupuncture charts. There were no markers or tissue changes along these pathways indicating any kind of anatomical channels.

"He even was able to measure the heat and energy along these pathways. Furthermore, he recruited yogis and other masters who were able to go into states of deep meditation to control their heart rate and metabolic rate. He painted liquid crystal diode suspension along their extremities and watched the meridians light up or go dark according to the masters' voluntary control of their autonomic nervous systems."

He specifically avoided the topic of the pain clinic dropouts and his discomfort at the air of secrecy in the clinic. But the other things he was sharing with Kaye (and nobody else) were all compelling ideas and experiences to this young explorer of the cosmos. Then one day he dropped by the pain clinic just for a visit. Soon he found himself in the conference room with the doctors, discussing energy medicine and expanded consciousness.

"You're an old soul," one of the doctors said. Then, almost in unison, they said to him, "There's someone we'd like you to meet."

# INFLUENCE (23 A.D.)

"So," Keene said, continuing once again where he had left off after their previous coffee meeting, "these professors introduced me to someone else. He's a philosophy professor at one of the local universities who teaches, among other things, metaphysics. I made a bunch of trips to talk to this guy. We talked about the concept of energy medicine. Telekinesis. Remote healing."

Keene related the encounters to Kaye.

"'What IS truth? Oh, you're a dangerous man, Doctor Dan.' This is what the philosophy professor always said to me, leaning back in his chair. He was always stroking his salt and pepper beard in the most wizardly fashion. He has this meerschaum pipe that dangles from the corner of his mouth. I kept waiting for him to drop it.

"After we talked all summer, this guy, Dr. Michael Woodward, Distinguished Professor of Philosophy, pointed his pipe in my face. He was half serious, half mocking. 'OK Doc,' he says, 'quit trying to convert me to Christianity!'

"'I wasn't doing anything of the sort. I was just asking questions,' I responded.

"Woodward had some strange adventures. He told me all about his explorations. He would go on and on about the mysteries of ancient cultures and how he had scaled the heights of Machu Picchu, explored the temples of Angkor Wat, celebrated along the banks of the Ganges at Varanasi at a Hindu festival. I mean, he meditated for an entire night, after bribing a security guard, in the middle of the Great Pyramid in the King's Chamber. Spent an entire night in there. Sounds scary to me. Imagine sitting in pitch black silence and feeling your soul leaving your body! Then he talked about this blue orb that would appear in his vision behind his closed eyelids after his guru brushed him with a peacock feather.

"I'm interested in all this stuff," Keene offered cautiously, his eyes looking distractedly across the coffee shop and back a little tentatively toward Kaye. "Ideas from all places East and West. All over the universe. Those clinic doctors showed me the teachings of this guru from India who had come to the West three quarters of a century before the Beatles made Maharishi Mahesh Yogi and Transcendental Meditation famous. I guess all this appeals to my curiosity. This guru quotes the Bhagavad Gita, Upanishads, Vedas, the Bible."

"You sure you're a Christian?"

He couldn't tell if Kaye was serious or facetious.

"Don't you think there's something that's not quite right about all this?" she asked.

"I guess somewhere inside I feel that something is wrong," Keene responded. "I guess I just have to know the truth. I do have these recurring dreams." Keene went on to relate the calf incident and the evil feeling of the black whirlwind. He told her about the tornado dreams and the particularly terrifying one he had had the night before he heard about his mom's terminal illness. He didn't tell her about the encounter with Alex. The experience was a little too fresh. "But there's so much more."

"Okay, go on." Her face betrayed … bafflement? Fascination?

"Well, Woodward introduced me to another guy who was doing a study on telekinesis or remote influencing. He's a PhD electrical engineer from Tech. Lives up on the Lake. He set up this study to test the idea of remote energy. You see, he built this greenhouse in his basement and planted a whole carpet of rye grass. Then he made little hair-thin servo arms to attach to the blades of grass. These were attached to extremely sensitive monitors that enable him to measure the growth rate of the grass in fractions of a millimeter."

"So?"

"It gets even more interesting."

"How is that even possible!" Kaye's head was spinning.

"There's this spiritual healer lady out of Baltimore who's a friend of Woodward's. She's kind of famous. She's written a few books about her life. She was born in a small Russian village and from an early age was a little bit like Snow White. No, really. When she walked into the forest, all the animals would gather around her." Kaye's eyes widened in curiosity. "She lives in the US now.

"She agreed to this experiment where she would, at a very specific time, send her healing energy to the grass. She's always very punctual and precisely at nine every Tuesday night she sends out her healing energy to her followers. Well, on the night in question two things happened. First, nothing. Then five minutes later there was a distinct upward spike in the growth rate of the grass. The engineer spoke with her the next morning and she apologized for her uncharacteristic tardiness. She had been delayed five minutes the night before.

"Oh! And I've met this other guy ..." Keene interjected, "but this one's top secret."

"Another one?" Kaye didn't know how to take all this in. "All right, please continue, do tell!"

At this point Keene was fearing Kaye was showing some real resistance. He couldn't tell. But he plunged on. "His name is Fred and he works as a security guard right here at the medical school campus. Fred is pretty ordinary, a real Southern country fellow. He has a healing ability. He told me in his heart of hearts he knows he was called to help and heal others. And he also agreed to cooperate with the doctors who were doing research on energy medicine.

"Fred's what you call an empath healer. He can sit with someone with an illness or pain, and when he touches them, he feels what they feel. Then he kinda just takes that pain into himself and the other person gets relief. Then he gets rid of his pain, or malaise, or illness somehow. Just like the death row inmate in *Green Mile*, only not so visual. Did you ever watch that movie?"

"Yup. Didn't like it much. Kinda creepy."

# FRED (23 A.D.)

The presence of Fred in the late-night halls of the university hospital had thrown quite a monkey wrench into the medical research various departments were doing. Clinical research coordinators were scratching their heads. They compared notes with each other across all departments. There did not appear to be any pattern. All departments were affected, from oncology to surgery to infectious disease. From neurology to endocrinology to pathology. They noted that in many of the ongoing trials, a statistically significant number of unexpected cures had occurred randomly and suddenly, thus skewing their data badly.

It was reaching a crisis level since outcomes data were statistically way beyond what was to be expected. Serious research dollars from the pharmaceutical industry were at stake. The Emory medical school data were under serious scrutiny. If the school's data couldn't be trusted, the cash infusion from pharmaceutical companies would be cut off. The only common denominator was as yet undiscovered. It was Fred. Keene had the privilege of a ringside seat as Fred did his thing.

"Come over here, Doc." Keene was still unfamiliar with being called by that title, especially since he was still just a student. But he followed Fred's lead.

"This is Ms. Bailey. She's got cancer in her liver, and it hurts. When I get close to her, my liver hurts, too. They're giving her some new drug they're testing. I don't think it agrees with her. We have been talking about things and she wants me to touch her. That still okay, ma'am?"

The pinched, pale yellow, frail-looking middle-aged woman nodded silently. Keene observed breathlessly. For about five minutes, Fred rested his hands lightly upon the woman's abdomen. He closed his eyes. His mouth moved in silent prayer. His face, once calm and peaceful, now slowly drained of its color, and his formerly placid countenance was replaced by a gaunt and pale-yellow visage etched with lines of agony. He removed his hands and collapsed into the recliner chair next to the hospital bed. Another five minutes passed that seemed like an eternity to Keene.

"What if a nurse comes in and sees what's going on?" he thought, slightly panicked.

Then Fred stirred. The color had returned to his face and he expelled a deep sigh. Ms. Bailey slept. Her ragged breathing was now soft and regular. The color had returned to her face as well. The yellow had faded a bit.

"We best be getting along now," said Fred.

Just then Keene's fear was realized. In walked the charge nurse, who had noticed the sudden calming of her patient's heart rate on the telemetry monitor.

"What are you doing in here, Fred, with this student? It's two-freaking-o'clock in the morning, and shouldn't you be out there on your rounds?" She directed her angry attention at

Fred. Then she glared suspiciously at Keene. "And you, don't you have some admissions or scut work to do?"

She swept them both up with her scolding, shooed them out of the room, then went to attend to Ms. Bailey who, though she was sleeping deeply, looked decidedly better than she had earlier in the night.

This scene, minus the incursion of the charge nurse, was repeated in other rooms, with other patients, when Keene was on duty and Fred took him in tow.

"Fred," Keene whispered loudly as he corralled Fred in the stairwell, having made their hasty retreat from the oncology unit. "You, we are going to get in some serious trouble. I don't think you're supposed to be in patients' rooms, and me, I'm not supposed to be there either unless I'm assigned to them. If we're reported, you lose your job and who knows what happens to me."

"Well, Doc. What am I going to do? There's people dying up here. And I can do something about it."

"I don't get it, Fred. Where does this power come from?"

"Always had it, Doc. I don't know. It sort of runs in the family. My momma could pull pain out of people. My daddy could stop bleeding from a cut by rubbing his hands over it. Doc, you and me are both Christians ain't we? I don't look on this healing thing as something that is downright supernatural. I think everybody has some kind of gift or power. I call it part of the natural order of things. Just that people nowadays don't want to believe humans have ability to see things without their eyes or know things without being taught, or make things change or move with just their thoughts.

"Doc, if you believe the Bible, then you should know Adam had all power from the beginning. No, really. He just started to lose it when he said no to the Almighty. Heck, Doc, he named all the animals in the world in a day. He was given the order to rule the world; that means the *universe*! Haven't you read Romans chapter eight? '... the whole creation groans for the revealing of the sons of God.' Why? Because the world's been falling apart ever since Adam fell. I believe the Bible says it's 'subject to futility' or something like that, right? Those Sons of God? That's *us*!

"Hey, Doc, did you ever stop to think how all these folks in the past could make things today we can't even come close to? We can't make any pyramids. We don't even have the machinery to move rocks like that, much less cut 'em and fit 'em together without cement. We didn't know the positions of stars and galaxies that folks thousands of years ago had figured out and wrote about on the walls of their temples until we had our giant telescopes and supercomputers.

"Ain't no such thing as macroevolution, nah! All the animals we see today didn't just evolve from lower forms. There were lots more animals thousands of years ago. And their DNA was chock-full of all the information needed to produce the offspring we see today. And folks a long time ago were lots smarter than now. Adam was perfect, just like the Bible said—'very good.' But he went off and blew it—'died,' the Lord said, on the day he ate that fruit. Don't get me wrong. People kept a lot of that power for a long time, but it faded away slowly. And there's a trace of that power still around today in some people ... like me.

"Now, Doc, I don't take no credit for it. It's a gift. Just read those healings in the Gospels. A lot of the time the Lord addresses someone who was healed seemingly spontaneously or someone else was healed because they asked Him. Did Jesus say that HE himself healed them? Well, yeah, but sometimes he says, 'YOUR faith has made you whole.' Now don't you think he was trying to tell us something about the gifts that he has given some of us? I'm just blessed to be one of 'em. And so are you, Doc."

# UNION (23 A.D.)

"OK, Kaye-girl. Dish it!" Her nursing buddies who lived on campus pressed around her to extract the truth. They were enjoying a little midweek wine and cheese up in the dorm.

"Is he a good kisser?"

"Hold on, now! We're just having coffee together!"

"Oh, come on, he was stalking you last month and now you're just having coffee with him?"

"No, it's not like that … Well, yes, he was kind of following me out on the trails, but he's really cute … and strange. We haven't even had a date. He hasn't asked me out. We've just been talking about a lot of stuff, philosophical stuff. He's different. Not like those other medical students that you guys are chasing!"

"Touché!"

"But I do like him. Wish he would ask me out. But he scares me a little, too. He has a lot of strange ideas. He's kind of like a little boy playing with dynamite. I think as much as anything, I feel like I need to, well, protect him. Just wish he'd ask me out."

"So, tell me about this boy," Kaye's mom said one evening. "I thought you were not going to nursing school looking for a husband."

"Mom, I wasn't. I'm not. You sound like my girlfriends. They're like, 'Hey babe, tell me about the cute med student.'"

"Well?"

"OK, Mother, he was sort of stalking me on the running trails."

"That's weird, honey."

"Not really. He's kind of shy, really. We've had coffee together a few times. He's different from the other med students. Goes on and on about philosophical things. He's really smart but doesn't brag about stuff. He's not hitting on me. Frankly, I wish he would."

Her mother smiled and expelled a sigh of mock exasperation.

✯✯✯

As the second year of medical school ground along, Keene was alone in his apartment one lonely weekend while others in his class were out partying. Keene paced restlessly around, with nowhere to go. In his mind an old Cat Stevens song was playing in his head: "Another Saturday Night and I Ain't Got Nobody …"

His phone rang. "Hello?"

"Hi, Danny?"

"Yeah."

"It's Kaye." She was taking the matter into her own hands.

"Well, yeah. I kinda recognize your voice."

"I was thinking maybe we could meet somewhere for a drink or something?"

His mind was screaming, "Oh, HELL yes." Instead, he said, "That's a fine idea, but let's not meet. I'll pick you up!" That was about as much control as he could muster.

"But you know I live way up in Buford …"

"No matter, I'm coming. Tell me how to get there."

So, he did. And they did. They had a drink or two at a cool live-band saloon featuring a group at the time that covered his favorite oldies, especially The Allman Brothers.

And all the time, as she sat across the small table from him and they talked, he leaned closer and closer. He was digging her more by the minute. He was thinking, "That smile and those eyes, those lips. That laugh and the quirky things she says. Liking everything I'm seeing from top to gorgeous bottom."

He took her home, but they stopped at the railroad tracks that ran through town. Yes, her house with her widowed mother was definitely on the *other* side.

"Hey, let's put a penny on the tracks," she said. "The train'll be by in a few minutes."

So, they put a penny on the tracks to let the train run over it. But they never found that smashed penny. Never even looked for it. They were too busy kissing. Now she could honestly answer her girlfriends with an enthusiastic "Yes, great kisser!" The dating began in earnest.

Keene blew it at Christmas. He was going home for the holiday, and Kaye took him to the airport to see him off. She had a gift for him. He didn't have one for her. He never lived that one down. But over Christmas, he knew that he knew. He came back and professed his forever love. She reciprocated.

They were married six months later. Until then, it was a winter and spring of snatched encounters and weekend dates in the midst of their jointly overwhelming academic and study schedules. They ran together as much as possible through the campus, the surrounding suburban streets, and the Gardens. They talked about marriage, a year-long engagement, and all those details. But they had friends, lots of them. There couldn't be a big wedding. They were poor. And by summer, passion was getting the best of them.

"Let's be married tonight!" Kaye whispered breathlessly between kisses. "We can do the ceremonial details later …"

"But … But … We're not officially MARRIED," he protested weakly. Kaye undid her top two buttons, then undid his.

"Okay, your turn," she teased him, directing his hands to the rest of her buttons, then around her sinewy back.

He fumbled at the little bra clasp, with one hand, then two. He gave up.

"You're not very good at this are you?" she grinned suggestively.

"I don't get any practice!"

"Well, we're going to take care of that, Danny-boy."

"No! No! No! Not yet. Just wait, just … wait!" he said breathlessly. "Just hold on a couple of days. We can go get our marriage license, go to the courthouse, then celebrate it with our friends, family, and church later. I'm the last one to be a rule follower. You know that. But this is one rule we won't regret following."

Kaye bit her lip, pouted, and sucked in a deep breath in mock dejection. Her face was flushed as she managed a frustrated smile. "Okay, Danny-boy. To the courthouse ASAP!" So, with giggles and sighs they made short work of restoring all the buttons to their original order.

The whole scene was rather inevitable. After all, Keene and Kaye had been with each other as much as possible for months. Now they suddenly announced their wedding plans to everyone with only two weeks' notice? Their explanation to friends and family was that clinical rotations would soon be starting and they knew they'd never see each other if they weren't officially married. It seemed a satisfactory reason to all. Thus, they had two weeks to put together a wedding.

Their friends secretly talked among themselves that she had to be pregnant.

# DARK SIDE (24 A.D.)

"What IS truth? Oh, you're still a dangerous man, Doctor Dan." The philosophy professor had taken this as his obligatory salutation to the young doctor each time he came for discussions. They had continued their conversations from time to time while Daniel was on clinical rotations near the university.

Daniel's mental and spiritual explorations led to his taking a couple of field trips. One of these was to the electrical engineer's house on the lake forty-five minutes north of the city, and he brought a reluctant Kaye along with him. The spiritual healer who had remotely made the engineer's grass grow faster was going to be there. She was "giving an audience" to a select group of "seekers." Things got strange and disturbing that night.

Daniel and Kaye were the last to arrive. The guests were assembled in a circular array of chairs in the large, cozy, rustic den. Fragrant logs sparked and snapped in the stone fireplace that occupied nearly an entire wall. The mingled aroma of sandalwood incense set a decidedly transcendental mood.

The engineer's wife warmly and affectionately ushered them in. There was one chair left to sit on. Kaye, as was her natural and generous bent, motioned for the hostess to take this last chair (all the men were sitting on the floor) and began to sit cross-legged on the carpet.

At that moment, the kind and serene countenance of the healer became dark. Her voice—which up to that point had been calm and mellifluous, laced with an accent of the Mother Country where she had been born—suddenly became a lupine bark. "Get up this instant! Sit in a chair like a lady!" The command was harsh, imperious, and stunning.

Keene, startled, looked at the Russian lady and was stunned by the transmogrification he observed. He stared intently in disbelief and bewilderment at the woman. For a moment, he saw (or imagined?) a dark formless orb or blob that seemed to obscure her face, much like a black theater scrim. And he distinctly smelled (or imagined?) the fragrant aroma of the sandalwood incense sticks now bore another scent, that of a dead rat somewhere in the wall; the rancid, smoky odor burned his eyes and nose. His mind went immediately to the bloated body of the dead calf in the mountain pasture. A shudder of revulsion overtook him momentarily and the memory of that evil, black-smoked pyre brought on a retch from his gut, which he quickly stifled.

Kaye was visibly shaken, the color drained from her face. She arose, with Keene assisting her, to another chair the engineer had quickly and obsequiously shuffled in. Then Keene sat at her feet, holding her ankle tenderly. The color that had left her face was rising in his, with pain, embarrassment, anger, confusion. Why had his wife been singled out in such a brutal fashion in the first two minutes of the encounter? It was nothing short of *demonic*, clearly. And the black haze that had appeared to Keene seemed to pulsate out from the healer in the direction of Kaye, never quite touching her but clearly reaching out in her direction. The putrid aroma persisted. Keene glanced around to see if anyone else detected it. There were no obvious indications anyone perceived something amiss. It seemed a visual and olfactory hallucination that was beyond disconcerting.

They didn't stay for the finale of the evening, which was to be a guided visualization led by the healer. Keene made excuses to the host, who perceived rightly it was Kaye's discomfiture that had prompted their early exit. The hostess didn't help things, with her parting words to the effect of "some people's minds just aren't open yet."

"Why did you take me there?" Kaye fought back tears.

"I—I'm so sorry."

"She was … evil."

He didn't want to acknowledge it, but somewhere deep down he felt it. Nothing further was said on the ride home.

Something else transpired that night. As he sat cross-legged in the darkness on the bed while Kaye slept fitfully beside him, he sank into a deep meditative state. At first, he thought he was just imagining someone else was in the room. But the presence of someone—some thing—else approaching the foot of the bed in the gloom grew more palpable. He saw nothing. Nevertheless, even though he sat in near-total darkness, the edge of the bed seemed more obscured from his vision than the remainder of the bedroom. The dark amorphous blob that periodically took a human outline inched across the bottom of the bed and ever so closer to Keene and the slumbering Kaye.

The usually contrasted pattern of the bedspread became indistinct. What had been a black-on-white toile pattern—a bucolic scene of cows, farm boys and girls, stone walls, and chickens—seemed to blend as the mist passed over. A creeping, hair-raising foreboding rose from Keene's spine and sent an uncomfortable tingle across his scalp. Again, the smell of smoke and a dead animal invaded his nostrils. A sinister, barely audible, and incomprehensible voice like that of tinkling water or shattering crystal hissed in the darkness.

Not knowing what else to do to rid the place and himself of this entity, imagined or not, he quietly but firmly rebuked whatever it was the only way he knew how ... in the name of Jesus. It disappeared.

After that, Keene hid his delving into Eastern spirituality from Kaye. Against her pleadings, yet strangely compelled, he plunged ahead into the mysteries of supernatural healing, wherever it came from. He stayed up in the library stacks late at night after rotations or studying, locking himself in the pitch blackness and silence of the private study rooms. He practiced the deep meditation techniques he was learning from a yogi's fellowship group. He asked the deep questions of how all these things could make sense together. Surely Jesus was his Master. Where did all this other stuff fit? And why had that supposedly wise, kind, and spiritual lady gone off on his dear Kaye? What—*who* was the black thing that continued to come and go in his life?

All of this the young doctor carried with him through the end of medical school and later on into his residency in family practice: a head full of knowledge and endless curiosity, a heart full of love for people, and hands that could feel something ... else. It was energy. That force coursing through every human body and the entire universe. He had felt it.

"Kaye, please don't be such a skeptic," Keene protested to Kaye. "Cynical people say it just feels good to touch another person because that's the chemistry of humanity. But it doesn't *always* feel good. When you genuinely like someone and feel love and compassion for them, a touch on the arm, or the back, or the cheek feels good. Is that just emotion? A physiological reaction? I don't think so. And if there's animosity or distrust? What do people say? 'Don't you dare touch me!'"

"I'm about ready to say that to you, dear"—Kaye's body language was saying it all—"and I'm not really a skeptic, Daniel. I just think there's a dangerous line you're crossing over."

There was another cloud. Not the inky reeking one; a metaphorical cloud. Sweet Kaye adored him, not totally understanding her husband who was so "out there" in his thinking. She loved him all the same through his clinical rotations in medical school and even in his absence. He was forever in the hospitals, slaving away. Learning what he had to learn. Seeing what he had to see.

The first night they had gone out together, they had talked and talked about everything. Kaye had been apprehensive at first, even though she had initiated that first "date." But during the evening leading up to that first kiss, she had been enraptured by the young doctor-to-be, with his knowledge of the Bible, his boundless curiosity to figure things out, and his belief that everything could fit into a unified philosophical framework. But still …

It wasn't the endless hours he spent in school that made him absent. Nor later the grueling hundred-plus hours a week of residency. Nor on top of that, the exhilarating yet bleak uncertainty of how to get started in the real world, being raw, untested, and saddled with debt.

Keene had been so preoccupied; he'd been reading books (not just medical texts) and studying arcane literature (most of it Eastern) expounding upon the energies of the universe and of the human body. He would stay up late and meditate for hours, letting his thoughts dissipate and losing awareness of his body. Kaye didn't understand it. But she loved him. Missed him.

"I wish you'd stop all this weird stuff, Danny." Kaye crossed her arms tightly across her chest and turned her back on him.

"But ... but sweetheart, there's just so much out there to learn and to know. I'm sorry, but these medical school nerds are just stuck in a view of the world that's less than half the picture. I'm just not ... just not one of them."

She heard the whimper in his voice, the little boy. She turned around to see him standing there, head bowed, shoulders slumped. She imagined the words in her head she wasn't yet ready to hear him say: "Honey, I'll throw all this stuff out the window if you want me to walk away from it."

She just wrapped her arms around him and held him close. She didn't have the heart, or the nerve, to shatter his passion.

# INTRODUCTIONS (24 A.D.)

Kaye and Daniel walked across the campus after catching lunch with each other. Drs. Bruno and Samin crossed their path.

"Hello, Daniel," they said in unison.

"Could this be the lovely wife you've never quit talking about?"

Kaye was not feeling very warm and flattered by this compliment from the pair who seemed to have considerable influence over her spouse.

"Yes, gentlemen," Keene said formally. "This is Kaye. And Kaye, this is Dr. Bruno and Dr. Samin." He gestured with a nod in their respective directions.

"We see great things in your husband's future," Dr. Bruno interjected. "He's so much more *progressive* than anyone else we've met in this medical school." Keene blushed a little and acknowledged him with a slight nod of embarrassment, and a bit of pride. Kaye's face turned slightly red as well, but for a different reason.

"Oh, we're so glad to see you because we have a real treat, a privilege to extend to you and your beautiful wife," Dr. Samin said.

"Oh?" Kaye muttered in feigned interest, suppressing her loathing at the obsequiousness of the pending invitation.

"Yes!" exclaimed Bruno. "Emory is having a gala. Not just any gala. An A-list gala of academic, pharmaceutical, and government officials to celebrate the incredible advancement of medical science in the drug industry. The leaders of major medical universities and research institutions will be there. The heads of the FDA and CDC. Top executives in the pharmaceutical industry. Even the chairmen of NIH, WHO, and the secretary of HHS!

"We've been invited due to our assistance in researching pain pathways and the manner in which innovative compounds can affect the awareness of pain; it might also be due to the fact that we're right here at Emory. But, still, it's a great honor."

"And we're each able to bring a plus one." Samin continued his partner's sentence without missing a beat. "That would be you Daniel, and you, Kaye?" He smiled broadly and spread open his palms ever so slightly.

"That sounds so cool," Daniel blurted.

"NOT COOL, Daniel." Kaye was furious at her husband's quick acceptance and told him so as they parted from the pain doctors. "There's something *dark* about them. Like that—that awful woman."

After the encounter with the doctors, Keene was even more eager to attempt to build a bridge between where he had gone in his quest and where Kaye stubbornly remained, refusing to budge. He arranged for his recalcitrant spouse to meet Fred.

"Hello, Kaye. It's so fine to finally meet you. Dr. Daniel has told me so much about you. And you are so pretty!"

"Thank you, Fred. Good to meet you," Kaye offered politely and cautiously, not sure she was liking the instant flattery, but feeling a bit better than she had after the previously offered compliments.

After initial pleasantries, Fred said, "Dr. Dan tells me you're not particularly happy with, well, the whole issue of divine healing."

"It's not just that." She hesitated. "Oh well, I might as well just come out with it. Fred, some of these things—or maybe it's some of these people I've met—seem, well, *evil*. I mean, not *you*, Fred. You don't feel that way." She was pondering how her foot was tasting at that moment. "You struck me as really nice from the second you opened your mouth," she said, backpedaling as fast as she could.

Keene sat quietly, listening intently, expectantly.

"That's OK, honey. Look, a lot of me is hard to explain. Let me try. Did your husband tell you that I got a divinity degree, and I used to be a preacher?"

"He said something about that."

"Well, I've always had this healing gift or power in me, from when I was a little boy. And I always wanted to preach the Gospel. So I left town to get an education before I came back to be a preacher."

"What town was that?"

"I'm not telling you that, or anyone else for that matter. Let's just say it was a long time ago in a place even more 'southern' than here." He provided the air quotes. "Things didn't work out there. So, I ran away."

"Ran away?"

"Yeah. Even changed my name."

"Why on earth?"

"Because the hometown folks came to hear me preach and teach ... but what they really wanted was for me to touch them and heal them. It kinda got out of hand because I wanted to tell the story of the Bible and tell the Gospel more than anything. But all the people wanted was a sign, a miracle. But what they were all just doing was throwing baby Jesus out with the bathwater."

Kaye smiled and suppressed a chuckle at that remark. Fred went on to explain his leaving his town and why he had needed to disappear as completely as he did; some of his former townsfolk and even church members had grown positively vindictive and even hostile.

"It was the darndest thing, Kaye. I even thought someone there might murder me. Something more going on there than just a simple disagreement. It was dark, really dark, Kaye. There is another side to this healing thing which isn't necessarily *good*."

"What do you mean, 'not good?'"

"Well, Jesus meant for healing to be a sign. A sign points to something, you know, gives directions. So, there's such a thing as a counterfeit sign. What I'm saying is that healing power can be used to deceive someone, you know, to direct someone away from the true healer. The one way to determine whether the healing power is good or evil is the message it brings. If it points you to your own power, it's not good. But if it points you to Jesus, that's the Truth."

Fred went on to explain the truth of scripture to Kaye as he had to Daniel; how he ended up in Atlanta working as a security guard, keeping his preaching and teaching under cover and really speaking about the things of faith to people one-on-one; and his healing that he practiced, as he said, "as the Lord leads."

Keene hoped that this encounter would alleviate his bride's discomfiture some. He was only partly right.

## GALA (25 A.D.)

"Okay, okay. Let's do it. After all we'll be leaving this place and these people soon; maybe not soon enough. But what'll I wear? You'll have to rent a tux and I'll have to scrounge up an evening gown. How can we afford that?"

But afford it they did. Keene got the tux. And Kaye found the perfect dress at a consignment shop. It was a gown that had to have been mistakenly and incredibly underpriced.

There she stood, the picture of grace and elegance. She was a deep turquoise vision in satin that conformed to her curves, with a sweep of navy-blue sequins adorning her front and back in artful crescents, which accentuated her lithe figure. Voile ruffles at the hem and along the split extending to her mid-thigh balanced the same look that framed her graceful bare shoulders, upper back, and impossibly beautiful neck. Capping it all off was quite a bit of bling, courtesy of a couple of rich nursing school mates who, upon seeing the dress and their friend, quickly volunteered bracelets, dangly earrings, and a necklace that framed her face and long blond hair, which was not in her usual ponytail but in a fashionable coif held together by another shiny silver and sequined comb.

Later in the evening, after they had spent some time at the event, more than one head had turned as Kaye and Keene crossed the marble floor of the event hall in the Fox Theatre. Kaye was a little uncomfortable. "Daniel, I think there's a wee bit too much décolletage here? People are staring at my boobs. Especially that guy over there." She nodded discretely in the direction of a dark-haired, svelte, and dashing man standing by the champagne fountain. He wore a finely tailored suit of Italian wool that broadcast his status and his athleticism.

Keene had seen him across the hall talking to Kaye earlier when she had approached the champagne. Keene had been procuring some delicacies from the oyster bar. Drs. Bruno and Samin were there next to this man, obviously making an introduction between him and Kaye. They had looked over and gestured in Keene's direction and the man acknowledged the distant husband with a polite nod. Keene felt distinctly uncomfortable as he strolled in as casual a manner as he could muster across the floor to his wife, whom he had seen recoil ever so subtly as the "hunk in the suit," as they referred to him jokingly later, touched her bare arm.

"Ah, Doctor Keene." It was Bruno who spoke. "Johannes, this is the medical student I told you about. He is a most promising young man. He's so far ahead of his peers in his ability to *understand* things." Bruno had lingered mysteriously over that phrase.

"Daniel, um, Doctor Keene, this is Mr. Johannes Akhtar, chief operating officer of Pelzer Pharma. We work directly with him in our joint research."

"It's a pleasure, sir, and thank you for the endorsement," said Keene, turning his face in Bruno and Samin's direction. "Um, sorry honey, but Dr. Kaplan, my favorite professor and chief of neurology, is begging to meet you," he said to Kaye for the benefit of Akhtar and the doctors. "If you'll excuse us?"

"Certainly," they demurred politely in sync.

✫✫✫

"Tell me about this young man," Akhtar inquired of the doctors as Daniel and Kaye walked over to Dr. Kaplan.

Samin spoke first. "He's a most perspicacious student. He sees things in a different way from other students who have rotated through our clinic."

"In what way?"

"Unlike his fellow students," Samin said, "young Daniel there sees a bigger picture. He's not captive to the narrow view. And he's particularly skilled at the injection procedures we have taught him, the paracervical sympathetic blocks. By the way, we're seeing some impressive pain reduction results with the addition of PX 91 to the regimen." He continued in the most ingratiating fashion. "We are delighted to be able to contribute to the advancement of research in this area and are grateful for your support. The backing of Pelzer Pharma has substantially improved the research in our department. I should take this opportunity to extend my thanks on behalf of the university."

Akhtar nodded politely and glanced over at Keene and his wife across the room. "Has young Doctor Keene taken note of any of the unexpected effects of the drug?"

Bruno spoke. "All of the staff are blinded to the exact composition of medications administered, so I strongly doubt Keene has any clue. Although he does seem to have established quite a rapport with a number of the subjects, er, patients in the clinic."

"That being said," Samin interjected, "he is quite an engaging young man. I hadn't had the opportunity to bring this up until now, but he has spent extra time interviewing patients lately. I wouldn't be surprised if he has uncovered some unusual effects in his discussions with them."

"Neither of you have discussed these things in his presence?" Akhtar asked.

"Oh, no," said Bruno a bit nervously. "We wouldn't be so indiscrete. But I do think it would be most prudent to shield him from any mention of this topic."

"Be sure that you do. Because I do desire to continue our support of your research." Having fired that warning shot over the pain doctors' bow, Akhtar pivoted stiffly, snatched another glance of Keene, and walked away.

"Thank God you got me away from them, from HIM," Kaye said. "He was hitting on me right in front of you! And he was, just, well, *dark* and creepy … like them!"

Keene glanced back over his shoulder as they approached Dr. Kaplan. The three men seemed as though they were in a huddle of sorts by the champagne. He noted Akhtar's glances in his direction. Blinking once or twice, Keene found it hard to make out their faces for a moment, that corner of the hall seemingly having lost its overhead lighting, which heretofore had lit up the area like the rest of the dazzling room. A dark, smoky shade obscured the area. Was he just imagining the smell of a dead animal?

# REPENTANCE (26 A.D.)

After the gala, and after saying goodbye to medical school, Keene and Kaye went off to the city and hospital where he would do his residency and she would be a nurse. Daniel Keene knew now something was seriously wrong in his soul. "The gut don't lie," his grandma used to say. And Keene's was screaming at him.

Keene reflected upon his undergrad days at that southern university. Although nominally Baptist, the school marched lockstep with the rest of contemporary university academia and was decidedly liberal. The entire mainstream of academia followed in the rationalistic footsteps of the Enlightenment: Hume, Kant, and a host of other philosophers. Keene had studied them all.

He had been led by the nose by historic figures such as Spinoza, as well as the Bible scholars (German, most of them), who would generally be lumped into a group who practiced higher criticism. Their primary aim was to demythologize the Bible; that is, to separate its devotional significance from its verifiable historical context. This meant parsing the text, analyzing the *Sitz im Leben* (life situation) of the ancient writers according to the assumptions of modern archeology, geology, and a decidedly Darwinist view of history.

The net result of these Bible courses that followed in the "higher criticism" of Wellhausen, Bultmann, and the like was to separate him from the childlike passion and enthusiasm for the Word of God he had had in his early teens.

Of course, there had been Fred, who, despite his decidedly rural presentation, had turned out to be unexpectedly erudite on the topic of Biblical Truth. So, as he drove home from the hospital late one night in residency, with Fred's words echoing in his head, Daniel recalled his own "fork in the road" event in college after his mother's death. "Did I take the wrong fork?" he thought. "But what could I have done but trust the academics, intellectuals, experts, and scholars who went before me? I mean, I'm a Christian and all that. But the Bible, like other Spiritual Books, being the Word of God, isn't literally true, is it? Though it *did* contain the highest of all Spiritual Truths, at least for me.

"Okay,"—he continued his inner conversation—"in college, I was wrestling with some life decisions. One day as I walked across that campus I was thinking: 'If only I lived in the actual *historical* world of Noah, Abraham, Isaac, and Jacob.' But these were just pieces of Hebrew mythology that contained, at best, the core of Spiritual Truth, right? It was not exactly a 'come to Jesus' moment for me. Just the opposite."

Now, a lifetime later, it seemed, he drove down the road from the hospital where he was training. He was drained from seventy-two straight hours of doctoring in a brutal environment. He was reflecting on one of those books Fred had given him, a book about Creationism, the Flood, and the geological theory of catastrophism. He pondered the fact that worldwide geological findings matched the Biblical approach much better than an Old Earth evolutionary view. The Young Earth Creationist view was so much more logical than the evolutionary ideas he had always held. But the theory of evolution, as old as Aristotle, had become the normative view of the whole Western world; it was Truth to the academic community from the middle of the eighteen hundreds. By the early twentieth century, it became the prevailing paradigm to most literate people.

So, why was he now open to a literal Biblical world view, a view he had rejected long ago? As strange as it seemed, it was all because of the soul-freeing, mind-expanding experience of deep meditation he entered in his late teens and early twenties. This experience, along with his philosophy courses, had enabled Keene to shed all preconceived notions of reality and the universe and to reject the philosophical materialism and the dogmatic assumptions of so-called "empirical science." For the first time in his life, he now had a truly open mind, free of the presuppositions of so-called "scientific" inquiry. He understood he had been led astray all his life by philosophical preconceptions, not scientific ones. As such, he had forever failed to recognize his own preconceptions and therefore had so easily swallowed the "party line."

"Hey, Doc, you gotta get outside of your so-called 'scientific' box!" Fred had implored him. Keene was still astounded at the volumes of information this country-boy security guard could impart on such a technical level. It was this unlikely man who helped him see that the historical, archeological, geological, biological, anthropological, and cosmological data that had filled his mind made sense only in light of the Biblical record.

"Hey, Doc, did you know that before the nineteenth century, the great scientists, like Isaac Newton, all believed that the

# UNREPORTABLE EVENT

Bible was *real history?* The reason Western science departed from believing in the Bible had nothing to do with science or new data. Among other places, the disbelief festered in the halls of the Royal Geological Society in London in the early to mid-nineteenth century.

"Yeah, just to be 'scientific,' these gentlemen of the Society could not stand using an ancient Hebrew text that was, in their minds, a bunch of myths and legends. They just didn't think it was right to think there could be—what do you call it?—a 'first cause.' To them, believing in a 'mythological' text defeated the purpose of finding out the way things are and the way things work. They wanted to erase God from the conversation.

"Never mind that geologists up to that point had all agreed the Bible Flood was responsible for all these layers of rock they were looking at. But now they had a new theory, and this one would make them basically kick out good scientists who were Bible believers. One of their guys drilled in sea beds in the mouths of rivers. He looked at all the layers; thousands upon thousands of them in the rocks. So, he came up with a theory called 'Uniformitarianism.' That means these rock layers were formed slowly by a uniform process over hundreds of thousands or even millions of years, since every layer represented, in their view, a cycle of one year. Heck, don't you see that he had come up with a model for a really 'old earth?' Gave Charles Darwin a kick-start in the pants!"

"What about the Grand Canyon, Fred?" Keene had asked.

"Why, just look what they say, Doc: that the Grand Canyon was formed over millions of years by the slow wearing down of the Colorado Plateau by the river. This rock also had been laid down over millions of years in some ancient ocean. Everyone today knows this, right? That's what science books teach, don't they?

"Nah, there's a much better theory: the Grand Canyon was formed over a matter of maybe weeks by a big crack in the Colorado Plateau. The plateau had functioned as a giant dam holding back a big ocean over the middle of what is now North America. That ocean was left over from the Flood. That little crack became a big one pretty quick. There's sandstone at the bottom of the Gulf of Mexico that has its start way up in British Columbia and up as far as Nova Scotia. There's a host of other things to back this up, Doc, contrary to popular opinion.

"And there's more. Did you know there's a pretty perfect small-scale model of the Grand Canyon, complete with buttes and cuts and layers? It was formed in about seventy-two hours when the dam that was formed by the flow from Mount Saint Helens broke. Spirit Lake flowed out just like the ocean had over North America. And it formed a pretty perfect mini Grand Canyon."

Keene had long since given up trying to understand the mystery of this man. Keene devoured so much in his reading about natural chronometers, geological and astronomical evidence of cosmic youth, and unredeemable inconsistencies in radiocarbon and other atomic decay dating techniques that were followed slavishly by modern science as proof of ancient age. And not to mention the glaring biological evidence that macroevolution, as it is taught, can't possibly occur due to the principle of irreducible complexity: that there's too much genetic information in even the simplest protein that must come together simultaneously for there to be any possibility that such a thing could happen apart from a pre-formed intelligent design. God.

"You gotta face the truth, Doc … that Book is totally true. God made everything in SIX DAYS! And did I tell you that there's really good physics to show that light don't behave the way we think it does? Yeah, like when we see a supernova on the other side of the universe, we're seeing it as it happens, in real time, NOT as something that happened ten billion years ago. The Creation is young; the Bible is TRUE."

"Okay, Fred, where did you get all this information?"

"Oh, that stuff? I read it in a bunch of other guys' doctoral papers when I was getting *my* own degree. And one more thing, Doc. Remember those books I gave you that prove there's order in the universe, intelligent design? Well, there's only two ways that could happen: one is that the universe evolved over time because of something like a 'divine mind' built into it. That would mean everything is God and the universe is headed toward perfection, in some kind of cosmic cycle. Kind of a Hindu view of things.

"The other is that a divine creator spoke it into being. It was perfect from the start but it's been going downhill ever since the Garden. So how do you tell if the power you see and feel in healing is good or evil? Like I said before, if the message that 'you are God' comes through, it's evil. If the sign points to Jesus, it's good."

Just then, a song came on the radio as Keene drove along, on a Christian station. Something like, "I'm Gonna Live Like a Believer." And the scales came off his eyes. It all made sense. This Book is Truth. From "In the beginning ..." to "Maranatha, come Lord Jesus!"

He pulled off the road and wept, went home, and chucked all the Eastern and occult stuff in the dumpster.

Keene walked slowly through the door, head held low and his eyes burning with tears. Kaye was seated on the sofa, a book in her hand. A cold supper sat on the kitchen table. She looked up and saw the stricken look on her husband's face and the sloping posture of his shoulders.

"Honey, what's wrong?"

"Oh, Kaye, I've been so far out there that I didn't realize how far I had gone. All this Eastern mystical stuff, no matter how profound it is or how accurately it seems to portray things, is just an evil distraction away from the one Truth. I'm telling you, sweetheart, that I'm done with all that. I threw away all those books." He wiped the tears from his eyes. Kaye took a tissue and helped him.

"I'm so terribly sorry," he said. "You have been right to worry about me. I need you." His head sank onto her shoulder.

"Well …" she lingered over the word, pressing his face tightly against her breast. "You just said, 'You were right all along, dear.'" She paused. "You have no idea how much I enjoyed hearing that. And you, my little Danny-boy, do you have any idea how sexy you are when you really need me?"

Holding his sweet Kaye close, he apologized again through bitter tears for all he had put her through. There were no barriers anymore to their oneness of soul and body.

The tornado dreams stopped that night.

# FAREWELL (27 A.D.)

A few months later, Keene once again sat across from the philosophy professor, not knowing it would be their last session. He made the only appeal he could possibly make. "Michael, Professor, please hear me."

He went on to explain his epiphany of how the Bible was the Truth, the only reliable Truth. Where it spoke of history, it was accurate. Where it spoke of spiritual things and principles for living, it was true. And most especially, how it stated that Jesus was not one among many. He was not just another in a line of "ascended masters" but the one and only Son of God, the Way, the Truth, the Life.

"You just asked me a while ago for the hundredth time in our conversations: 'What is Truth?'" Keene said. "It's really hard to tell these days, isn't it? You have the government, the media, the experts telling you that their version of the Truth is the only one, whether it be about the environment, global warming, or even the definition of male and female.

"Well, nowadays everyone seems to be proud to proclaim their acceptance of everyone else by saying 'you have your Truth and I have mine.' But how can that be, Professor? It is either true or false. You can follow the teachings of 'ascended masters' in the tradition of Hinduism or Buddhism. You can rely on ancient texts that are steeped in myth and legend with little connection to actual history. You can call that Truth. But is it? I don't care what heights of consciousness you attain, or what power you think you have acquired. What is the message? That you are God. That we all are if we but knew it to be true.

"But there's only one ancient text that is proven to be true to history and it's the Bible. It says there is one true God ... and it's not us. And there is one and only one Truth."

Not being one to carry tracts and engage in evangelistic preaching, Keene nevertheless appealed fervently in that moment to the professor, implored him to decide, to make a choice, one upon which the outcome of his soul depended.

"You know, Professor, you've experienced this 'expanded consciousness' and felt your oneness with the universe, but Jesus said, 'What does it profit a man if he gains the whole world and forfeits his own soul?'

"The word in Greek for 'world' is *Kosmos*, the universe."

The professor nodded. Then quite stunningly and unexpectedly, the dangling pipe fell from the corner of his mouth. The clay shattered on the floor, sending ashes and sparks across the tile and against the baseboard. He leaned forward, prostrate on his desk, his head rocking slowly back and forth.

Keene watched him in quiet anticipation.

The professor gathered his composure, raised his head. His face was pale. With a trembling hand he pulled out a piece of notepaper from his desk drawer. On it was a curious rune-like, calligraphic scrawl that Keene could not make out from across the desk.

"You've come here today, Dr. Dan, to appeal to me to make a decision ... right?"

"Well, yes, of course I am appealing—no *imploring*—you to do just that."

"Dan, if I thought you were just some closed-minded, dogmatic, peckerwood Bible thumper, I wouldn't give you the time of day, much less sit with you and listen now. But I know you. We haven't talked, what, for a couple of years now? I know you have thought, and I know how you think. And now you've come all the way back here today after being away awhile. And you said you felt compelled to drive downtown to tell me this very day to, quote, 'make a decision?'"

"That's about the size of it, sir." Keene held his breath.

"You see, Dan, I have this student in my class. She's, well, a witch. A medium. A channeler of spirits. She's smart. And just two hours ago she gave me this." He handed the notepaper across the desk to Keene. The quaint antique scrawl was appropriate to the message it contained. It read:

*Professor,*

*I have so appreciated your class. You have taught and shared with me so much. And now I have something that I must share with you.*

*You know that the spirit voices have been talking to me. And they have told me to deliver a message to you. In unison these last twenty-four hours they have been crying out to me to come to you to tell you that ON THIS VERY DAY, you must MAKE A DECISION.*

*I'm not sure what this means. But this is me telling you.*
*Your student,*
*Pandora Black*

"Seems like I'm getting a message from both sides, huh?"

"Yup. Seems so. So, what'll it be?"

No answer came that day. It was the last time Keene saw the professor. And, looking over his shoulder as he exited the room, he thought he saw the area over the professor's desk grow cloudy and dark. It wasn't from smoke coming out of that pipe; neither was the distinct aroma of charred, rotting flesh.

The last time Keene heard about the professor; he was reading the professor's obituary. He never knew what happened. But he knew what he feared.

✭✭✭

It was on that same trip back to Atlanta that Keene made a date to hang out and toss back a beer or two with a few of his med school friends. They had stayed behind to pursue specialty residencies at Emory. These guys had never passed up an opportunity to rib Daniel about his philosophical tendencies. He was about to give them a bunch more fuel for the fire.

"What do you mean, you believe in a Young Earth?" they hooted in unison. "Keene, you've finally committed intellectual suicide."

"Well, before we get into astrophysics, the speed of light, and all that stuff, why don't we tackle something a little closer to home, like microbiology, okay?"

"Where are you headed with this, Keene?"

"Stay with me, guys. Now how many amino acids make up the simplest protein?"

Silence.

"Okay, the answer is: around forty-four. Although there are twenty unique amino acids, they have to be put together and folded in a specific sequence to form a protein molecule. A peptide chain has between two and fifty amino acids.

"Now, arguing that these amino acids are easily joined together (which they're not) without any complicated pre-existing conditions to form the bonds, what are the chances that a unique and functional chain of amino acids can be formed randomly; that is, without reference to a divine creator, intelligent design, or what is called the principle of irreducible complexity?"

"Okay, so?"

"The chances of a functioning protein of fifty specifically sequenced amino acids coming together randomly are one in ten to the fiftieth. Let's just say that these pairings come together at the rate of one per nanosecond. Pretty fast, right? Yet the number of years needed for this sequence to come together by random processes exceeds the age of the known universe. This is ignoring the fact that in order for life to exist, a host of functioning proteins has to emerge simultaneously, thus rendering this event even more improbable.

"Oh, and what about that genetic code? Empirical observation points to the fact that increasing the order and encoding of new information, or 'macroevolution,' just can't occur. What we do observe is SNIPS, single nucleotide polymorphisms, or the loss of information with each successive DNA replication. And don't think that bacterial resistance to antibiotics is evidence for macroevolution. On the contrary, resistant bacteria are actually weaker than normal flora. It's just that they have lost genetic information that controls intracellular processes. These are the very processes that antibiotics interrupt to kill these germs. With these processes altered by the loss of genetic info, the bacteria are no longer affected by these antibiotics. Thus, it is defective and weaker germs that survive, not stronger, normal ones. So why do we persist in calling them superbugs?

"I can go on forever here, guys. So, let's switch over to radioactive isotope dating. I'll be brief here. You'd think that geochemists would dismiss these methods out of hand, since each of several methods calculates an age of the universe that differs from the others exponentially by millions or billions of years. Guess this kind of testing isn't so reliable, huh?

"So now, let's look at a real reproduceable experiment. Some Creationist geologists drilled down into the earth's crust to pull up samples from the base rock, supposedly laid down millions or even billions of years ago. Then they tested the samples for residual helium in the rocks. They sent the samples out to separate independent labs for analysis. Based upon the amount of helium in the shale samples, they independently calculated the age of the rocks to be between five and seven thousand years old. They determined this knowing that helium has a finite and known diffusion rate. Samples a million years old should have had no helium left in them. Surprise!

"Want more? Okay, try salt in the ocean. We know how fast salt is accumulating in the sea. At current rates, all of our oceans would be hundreds of times saltier than the Dead Sea or Great Salt Lake. That is, based upon our dogmatic belief that the planet's oceans are millions of years old.

"Or try the orbit of the moon. It's decaying outwardly each year and getting further from the planet annually. By about an inch. At the current rate it would have left the earth's orbit a long time ago ... Last time I checked, it was still there.

"There are hundreds more examples, but I'll finish with this one. We're told that the time since the Big Bang is around thirteen billion years. Now, the closest galaxies have lots of blue giant stars, the hottest and the youngest of the stars. We expect to see them in nearby galaxies but not in distant ones. We would expect to see this because they're burning up their fuel faster than other stars, and the time needed for their blue light to get to us is well within the fuel range of nearby galaxies but outside the range of distant galaxies. So, why is it that we see the same proportion of blue giants at the furthest reaches of the observable universe as we do nearby? This just can't be possible if popular scientific notions of cosmic age are correct. Sorry, did I say I'd finish with the last example?

"The Bible says that the earth is around six thousand years old and that it was destroyed by the Flood around forty-five hundred years ago. It didn't just 'rain for forty days and forty nights.' The narrative states that most of the water came up from below, the 'fountains of the Great Deep.' This was a geologic as well as meteorologic catastrophe, and the face of the earth bears ample evidence to this event. Current studies of the earth's crust using ground-penetrating radar technologies confirm that even now there is more water under the surface of the earth than in all the oceans combined.

"Okay, just one more thing; and this is my personal favorite. 'God saw the rainbow and remembered His covenant.' He would never destroy the earth this way again. Well, before the Flood, the earth was watered by a 'mist' rising from the face of the earth. No clouds and rain at that time. After the Flood, all that water in the atmosphere rained down. Only after that did the atmospheric conditions exist that would allow for the formation of a rainbow. The rainbow is the visible sign that there would never again be this degree of rainfall on the planet.

# UNREPORTABLE EVENT

"I'll spare you my thoughts on global warming." Keene grinned mischievously. "I mean, if ninety percent of scientists agree on a topic, it must be true, right? WHAT IS TRUTH, after all? Scientists have never been wrong, have they? So have you had enough? 'Cause I've got more."

"Time to cry 'uncle!'" they said, "and grab another beer!"

# UNCLE DAVE (28 A.D.)

Uncle Dave was a character. He had a thick Oklahoma drawl. He was a highly successful oilman, a wildcatter. Wildcatting is a risky business. Dave was half of a two-man partnership. His partner was the driller. He was the lawyer. The partner's job was to locate promising yet unproven areas to drill, usually on the periphery of known oil fields that were already taken up by major oil producers. Dave would secure the leases for these small patches of land. He also rounded up investors to share in the speculation. Both partners were good at what they did.

Uncle Dave was hospitable, well-read, jocular, and an excellent storyteller. His college roommate—a cookie-cutter image of Dave, having also been successful in the oil industry—had gone on to be a successful Hollywood character actor.

Uncle Dave had also been a daredevil chopper pilot in Viet Nam, the youngest one in the group. He had been decorated for courageous flying and the rescue of countless ground soldiers, and for braving heavy enemy fire on multiple occasions. He was a war hero with a healthy appetite for risk-taking. And at the age of seventy, he looked like he was fifty.

# UNREPORTABLE EVENT

Late in Keene's residency (after his epiphany), he and Kaye paid a visit to Norman, Oklahoma, to visit her mother's brother.

"Hey Danny!" The salutation dripped of Okie hospitality.

"Good to see ya, Uncle Dave!"

"Mind if I ask you a medical question?" Uncle Dave asked. Keene never minded. It's what he lived for.

"Go ahead."

"Well, I was having this, well, pain, or discomfort, or something right about here." He pointed to a spot to the right of and above his navel.

"I went to my doctor. They ran some blood tests and even did an ultrasound of my belly and over my liver. They said I was fine. What do you think?"

"The list of things that this could be is fairly long," said Keene. "I mean, from simple indigestion to an ulcer. Could be gallbladder issues. Let me ask you a couple of things."

After a lengthy interrogation, Keene said, "Uncle Dave, do you mind if I feel your belly a little bit?"

"Go for it, son!"

So, Dave stretched out on the couch while Kaye and Aunt Nadene watched curiously. Daniel ran his hands over Dave's belly, alternately compressing and releasing gently in each area, each quadrant. Nothing.

Then, the doctor elevated his hands a few inches above Dave's horizontal (if potbellied) abdomen. As he passed his hands slowly above his uncle's midsection, Keene felt a heat, an energy, a vertical column of pressure emanating from a spot to the right of and above the navel.

He'd felt this before.

"Uncle Dave, I think—no, I know—something is going on here. I think you'd better see another specialist or two. I'll be checking on you."

Then, the last Christmas before Keene and Kaye's launch into the "real world" after his residency, a package appeared at their doorstep. It was from Uncle Dave. Following Daniel's urging, Uncle Dave had consulted with another specialist who had looked in his stomach with a scope and put dye up in the ducts to his liver. They did a CT scan. It was pancreatic cancer. But it was small and very early. He had to undergo major surgery to remove it all, but he was cured!

They opened the package. There was nothing solid in it. But an envelope was nestled in the Christmas gift box stuffed with tissue paper:

*My Dearest Kaye and Dr. Dan,*

*I can't express enough my love and gratitude to you both. Especially to you, Kaye, my sweet niece who has somehow managed to marry the man who saved my life. Don't worry about what you're going to do next. Please accept this as a small token of my deep, deep thanks.*

Enclosed with the missive was a check for a million dollars.

"How'd you like to set up a practice in an antebellum town? I hear the community hospital out there is looking for new family doctors," Keene said.

"Sounds wonderful to me!" She leapt into his arms with a squeal of delight at the financial freedom that had just been given to them. She wrapped her legs tightly around him, surrounding and embracing him. Together, intertwined with sighs and moans of relief and anticipation, they tumbled onto the living room sofa.

# OFFICE (29 A.D.)

Nurturing a young medical practice as an independent doctor in a world of managed-care administrative and bureaucratic nightmares was tough enough. But Keene loved getting to know his patients, figuring things out, and making diagnoses that others missed. This gave him the energy he needed to sustain the administrative hassles. Still, it was very hard.

Life after residency had started off with the highest of hopes, plans, and aspirations. With no financial pressures and worries to impede their progress, thanks to Uncle Dave, they were able to set upon the task of finding a home and establishing an office practice. They had found both right on the same spot.

Except for a significant slowdown for over a year or so due to the nationwide panic over the COVID pandemic and the subsequent near shutdown of the foot traffic in his office, business was great. Keene had resisted the propaganda of the government, big media, big pharma, and the mainstream medical establishment regarding the nature, origin, and solution to the virus. He refused to be swept up in the hysteria and Draconian suppression of alternative opinions and solutions.

The words of Professor Woodward echoed in his head: "What is Truth?" These days it was hard to tell.

So, this was home and office, the carriage house beside the mansion in Madison, Georgia, the town that Sherman had bypassed in his scorched-earth invasion of the South. He had spared Madison due to the pro-Union sympathies of the congressman who represented the town at the time. This gentleman also happened to have ties with William Tecumseh Sherman's brother.

Just a couple of years into his practice, Keene's reputation had grown exponentially. It's one thing to be the new kid in town in an area that needed general practitioners. It's another thing to establish healing relationships with one person after another. Keene's reputation for compassion and curing grew quickly. Patients would share with one another what the young doctor could do with his hands:

"Betty! I told him I had an ache in my back that was keeping me from doing my quilting," Miss Doris gushed. "You know, if I didn't have that I'd have nothing." Betty had, of course, nodded approvingly.

"Well, he put his hand on my back and, I swear (oh dear, I shouldn't talk like THAT!), right on the spot. I hadn't told him where it was. In a couple of minutes, the pain went away. He wrote me a couple of prescriptions that, honestly, I didn't fill because the problem just went away. He was going to send me to a physical therapist, but I didn't need that either. And there's more! I just don't know; he's got this way of paying attention to you. I just started talking about things, the past, my daddy, my late husband, Harold, stuff like that, you know?

"I wrote him a thank you note. Ran into him at the hardware store the other day. Thanked him again. He put his hand on my shoulder and just laughed. 'You know it's Jesus who does all the healing,' he said.

"He doesn't have Bibles or tracts or crosses or anything like that around his office, but I swear (oops, I did it again)," she giggled like a schoolgirl, "that young man is special."

✬✬✬

In addition to establishing a medical practice, the happy couple scouted out the area and managed to find a church that suited their theology and style; specifically, Biblically solid with an enthusiastic contemporary worship. It wasn't particularly easy. After a few months of steady Sunday visits, they came upon a small but vibrant and growing young church led by a gentleman with an impressive if somewhat unusual resume.

Jonathan Andrews had received an undergraduate degree in religion with a minor in business, then gone on to obtain his Doctor of Ministries degree at a respected Southern Baptist seminary. The son of missionaries in Guatemala, he had been brought up in the jungles of Central America. He maintained a lifelong yearning to serve these people among whom he had grown up. Uniquely, he combined this desire to serve with an entrepreneurial spirit and a self-professed tendency to be a total coffee snob.

He developed a coffee business in the States for growing, exporting/importing, and roasting coffee to support Christian coffee growers in Guatemala, Panama, and other countries. The roasteries and coffee shops at various locations around Metro Atlanta (including Madison) each housed a local church. Proceeds from the shops, including the unique coffee infusion products that they developed and sold to restaurants and retailers, both supported the American churches and gave income to the Central American growers and workers in the groves. Each coffee plantation supported its own church congregation.

Kaye and Daniel were immediately drawn to Jon, who sported a partly balding head, biker beard, and gold earring. He preached the Bible Gospel and sang a mean tune. On more than one occasion, Daniel had the opportunity to discuss with him the side of spiritual life that most Americans did not deal with.

"Jon," Daniel asked over a latte in the shop of the church, "how often did you come face-to-face with 'the demonic' down in Central America?"

"Well, let's just say such things are much more out in the open down there than they are here. Third-world folks are more accustomed to dealing with things that would be considered superstition around here. That's not to say that the demonic realm is any less active in developed nations. It's just like the saying goes: 'The devil's greatest weapon is making everyone think he doesn't exist.' Why do you ask?"

Keene went on to relate his childhood experience of the farm, the calf, the smoky entity, the dreams. He told Jon of his deep dive into Eastern mysticism and his serious examination of healing and healers, about whether one could discern if there was a good side and a bad side to "supernatural" healing.

"I'll have to pray about this one, Dr. Dan. What I can say off the top of my head is that if the healing leads you to Jesus, the One True Healer, it's probably good. If it leads you elsewhere, well, it's not."

"Someone else I know told me the same thing," said the doctor.

✡✡✡

Kaye and Daniel would run together during lunch hour, or at the end of the day if work allowed, laughing and chatting as they ran. Just as they had in school and residency.

"So why are you wearing those shoes?" Kaye teased. "Pretty tacky …"

"Gimme a break, darlin' … y'know I'm an expert on shin splints. Took me forever back in med school to finally figure it out. Gotta have the right shoe to stop the pronation, y'know? I'm not as skinny as I was back in my cross country days."

"You can say that again, Fat Boy …"

"OK, you can stop it now, Sweet Cheeks …"

"Not gonna stop it, unless you can catch me, Fancy Feet …"

It was a heady and ecstatic time. Keene had been thriving in his work and position on the medical staff of the regional hospital. Kaye worked shifts there on the med-surg unit. They caught a little smooch time by the coffee machine when Keene made rounds.

And how they ran together! Worked up sweat and passion. Sometimes, when time allowed, they followed through on that, too. (Lunchtime was a wee bit rushed.) They were doing well despite the forced near shutdown brought on by the pandemic. Keene was beyond infuriated at the way so-called medical experts controlled the pandemic. Nevertheless, he kept the practice going and they continued their jogging and laughing.

But one day, one of Kaye's feet didn't quite move right in front of the other. Kaye took a dive.

"Ouch," she said, still laughing as she brushed the wood chips off her palms. "You gonna lay hands on me and make me feel better like you make everybody feel better?"

"Honey, you know there's special feel-better therapy that is reserved only for you!"

# UNREPORTABLE EVENT

# THE PRESENCE (23 A.D.)

Years earlier, a young medical student struggled to keep his eyes open and to maintain his balance as he stood at the back of the group of fellows, residents, and other medical students making rounds with the department chairman. He had been awake all night doing admissions workups on patients on this service. His efforts, of course, were superfluous to the actual care of the patients. The residents took care of that. The workups that medical students did were training exercises.

As he labored in vain to stay conscious, he leaned against the wall of the hospital corridor, eyes heavy lidded and knees starting to buckle. His semi-comatose inattentiveness was spotted by the chairman, who then took the opportunity to make an example of him, storming to the back of the pack and scolding Keene for slacking off. Then the chairman asked him a couple of medical questions pertaining to the case at hand. Keene, of course, could not come up with any answer to the technically obscure interrogation. The chairman's intent was to strike fear in the hearts of all present. Mission accomplished.

Now thoroughly awake, Keene dutifully tagged along in the holy procession into the next patient's room. Still smarting from the dressing-down he had just received, he pondered the formal and ceremonial aspects of "morning rounds." There was a clear hierarchy here, as reflected in the vestments of the participants.

The medical students wore short white coats with short sleeves, the emblem of the medical school attached to the shoulder. They were at the back of the pack, the lowly position of the acolytes. Next up the line were the interns and residents, who also wore short coats, but theirs were long sleeved. They were the priests in training. Occupying a more honored position at the head of the group and next to the chairman were the fellows, the junior priests. They had long white coats befitting their status as next in line to be attending physicians themselves.

The chairman wore a long white coat as well. He had a closetful. They were kept fresh and available to him by the hospital laundry service. The status of attending physicians in the school was evident to all, as their name, rank, titles, and department were clearly displayed in multiple lines of blue on their left breast pocket. The more lines of blue, the higher the rank.

Keene was the last to enter the room of the next patient, a middle-aged woman suffering from some mysterious ailment that, up to this point, had baffled the doctors. As the chairman and entourage surrounded her bed, she cowered beneath the sheets. Keene made quick note of her fear.

As the chairman pontificated on the esoteric medical issues involved in her situation, Keene could not help but see that the poor patient was being neglected. The conversation that was held over her and not with her seemed nothing more than ritualistic incantations. He kept his eyes on the patient. She spotted him also and fixed her gaze on the only one in the room who acknowledged her existence. The attending physician finished his soliloquy, and they exited the room. Keene lingered for a moment and approached the woman.

"Ma'am, did you understand anything that the chairman said about your condition?" he asked.

"No, Doctor."

"You know, I didn't either." He grinned wryly. "But I tell you what. I'll go find out what I can and come back and explain to you. If that's okay?" He patted her on the shoulder.

A broad and grateful smile broke out on her face. As Keene turned to leave, she said, "Hey, Doctor, you made me feel good just by being here. That's special."

✵✵✵

In later years, Keene remembered this incident, as well as other similar ones. One particularly interesting one was "X." That was his name, or at least the one given to him by the hospital, since he had no ID and hadn't volunteered any. Nary a soul had come forward to volunteer any information about this hideous being.

X had been transported in by EMS, having been dragged in half dead from some godforsaken back alley. He was septic. The technical term was "empyema;" his chest cavity (the space between lung and chest wall) was filled with a foul lake of pus. X was a fearsome creature. He was wiry and emaciated. His body was covered with scars from numerous knife fights. His left eye socket was empty, also the result of combat with blades. His open, snarling mouth revealed interrupted rows of black and broken teeth that appeared more bestial than human. Keene learned that the rotting dentition was the source of the severe infection that festered in his chest and had to be drained.

X was a snarling and vile facsimile of a human being, and he had to stay restrained by his ankles and wrists to the gurney and hospital bed, lest he throttle with his clawed hands any caregiver who ventured too close. It was Keene's good fortune to be assigned to this man.

Keene and a staff nurse were picked to assist a senior surgical resident in the process of inserting a chest tube to drain the infection from the chest cavity. As the scalpel penetrated the space between two ribs and invaded the pleural cavity, out poured the foulest and rankest gray stream of liquid. Before the resident could insert the drainage tube, an impossible wave of stench enveloped the trio. The nurse, though she had been seasoned by many disgusting encounters, immediately lost her lunch. Keene would have as well, but he had not eaten that day and the heaving of his gut produced nothing.

This was the patient to whom Keene was assigned for the next month. Such was the odor that emanated from his room on the pulmonary service that an entire wing of the hospital had to be evacuated. The fame of X spread, along with the smell, through the entire medical class, though few in the group were able even to get close to him. Keene, though, was strangely moved by this pitiful specimen, and he dutifully waded through the feculent fog twice a day to tend to him. Keene spoke kindly to him and braved X's grasping talons in order to get close enough to lay hands on him and pray.

On the last day of Keene's rotation on the service, he walked cautiously to X's bedside to say his goodbyes. X extended a gnarled hand toward the startled student, the padded restraint preventing him from grabbing his intended victim by the arm.

Unexpectedly, X uttered his first coherent words. "Hey, Doc. C'mere."

"What is it, X?" Keene responded tentatively as he edged a bit closer.

"I know you be leaving today."

"Yeah."

"I just wanted to thank you. I wanna shake your hand." He extended his claw toward Keene, as far as the restraints would allow.

"What? Why?"

"'Cause you be the onliest one what treat me like a human bein'. And, just so you know, my name is Leroy."

Keene sank down against the wall outside Leroy's room as he left. Overcome with guilt, compassion, and confusion, he wept.

Over the years of medical school, residency, and his growing private practice, his patients would always comment on Keene's "bedside manner." When he himself was in the position of mentoring medical students and residents, he created another term for this phenomenon of making patients feel better: "therapeutic presence."

He would often say, "If you've got it, work it!"

This "therapeutic presence" was something that Keene did use. He understood that, as Fred had repeatedly pointed out, it was something to be cultivated and nurtured.

"Everyone has a 'presence' of some sort," he explained. "Entertainers have a stage presence. Military officers and politicians have a leadership presence. Good teachers have a didactic presence. Counselors, an empathetic one."

But another kind of presence was making itself known in the early days of Keene's practice.

"I'm getting pretty frustrated with my clumsiness out there on the trails," Kaye confessed. "And I've had some thoughts and urges lately that just aren't like me."

"What is it, honey?"

"Well, you know I'm the last person in the world to give in to feelings of depression."

"You can say that again!" Keene responded. "I've never met a more positive person than you, dear."

"But lately," Kaye said softly, "I've had some dark thoughts. I mean, they come out of nowhere, mostly when I'm sitting around quietly. It's like a voice in my head. It talks about suicide." She hung her head. Keene pulled her close.

✯✯✯

Kaye and Keene had made friends with their neighbors, especially the attorney and his wife and three children who lived next door. Peter Johnson, the lawyer, was a mountain of a man, all six-foot-two, 260 pounds of him. Ex-marine. He was a fast talker, as brusque and self-confident as was befitting the criminal defense attorney that he was in downtown Atlanta. He was forever chomping on a cigar and pontificating on whatever political topic occupied his thoughts on any given day. He carried a .357 magnum and boasted, "If they know you're carrying the big gun, you're less likely to have to use it." Considering his clientele and the parts of town he frequented, it was an appropriate motto. He was an intimidating fellow that most folks steered clear of. Not Keene. He loved to sit with Peter Johnson, Esq., and talk with—well, *listen* to him.

One evening a most terrible thing occurred. Keene and Kaye were sitting and munching on leftover eggplant parmesan that she had made earlier in the week. The front door of the carriage house rattled on its hinges as someone pounded desperately upon it.

"What is it, Shelley?" Keene didn't have time to say more as the neighbor's daughter pressed across the foyer breathlessly.

"Come quick, Dr. Dan! I think Stephen has shot himself!" she sobbed.

Keene ran out the front door in hot pursuit as Shelley sprinted across the spacious lawns that separated his house from the Johnsons'. Peter met him at the foot of the staircase and they hurried up together. They ran down the hallway to the still closed and locked door of Stephen's bedroom. "You ready, Doc?"

Peter kicked in the heavy wooden door, fracturing the casing and latch that had heretofore been solidly impossible. The door swung violently inward to reveal the prone figure of the young man beside his bed. A pool of blood covered the floor adjacent to his head; a .357 magnum police special lay next to a lifeless hand.

Keene quicky knelt beside Stephen and tucked the young man's arm and shoulder under his body. Deftly reaching across Stephen, he rolled the prostrate form toward himself. A gaping wound on the right side of Stephen's temple became visible, extruding blood and gray matter. The open eyes were dull and without animation. Instinctively and without forethought, Keene bent lower toward the lifeless body as if to begin resuscitation efforts. A firm iron hand gripped his shoulder, pulling him back.

"Don't do it, Doc. It's no use. I've been in Ramadi and a lot of other bad places," said the tough ex-marine, choking back tears. He reached for the bedspread, pulled it off, and covered his son where he lay.

The story unfolded in subsequent days that Stephen had not been doing well in college. Although he had been holding down a job, it was just a poor-paying table-waiting gig. He was living at home and having money trouble. His girlfriend was breaking up with him.

He had left no note and had not betrayed any inclination toward suicide. Yet here he was. The circumstances of his life had descended upon him. A gun was available. The irresistible impulse had overcome him. And he was gone.

Over the ensuing weeks, Keene spent many hours sitting with Peter in the attorney's study. The attorney, as was his bent, pontificated without interruption on all topics economic, political, and theological while chomping furiously on his cigar. To the casual listener, it would have seemed that Peter was trying hard to instruct the doc, but Keene knew better. Peter was really asking questions.

What Keene couldn't say to Peter, even though he did have a couple of opportunities, was that he deeply suspected that Stephen's sudden suicidal urge had not come out of the blue. Hadn't Keene's own wife felt it just the day before? Although he didn't tell her at the time, Daniel also had felt it. And Stephen had succumbed to it.

Daniel remembered the evil at the mountain cabin, the dark presence that had seemingly pursued him in medical school, his tornado dreams, and the demon on the mental health center lawn that had been possessing that patient. He was all too familiar with the smell of trauma and blood, having spent thousands of hours in the emergency room. He was also familiar with the scent of burning, rotting flesh. He had once again caught a whiff of that scent in Stephen's bedroom that evening.

# OTIS (30 A.D.)

Otis Bennett flipped on the under-cabinet light that illuminated the work desk in the kitchen. It was the only light in the house he wanted to turn on, afraid as he was of awakening Sarah. He quietly slid open the desk drawer and produced a zebra-striped, bound academic notebook. Glancing at the clock on the stove, he noted the time: 3:00 a.m. There would be no more sleep for him tonight, just as there hadn't been many well-rested nights since Doc had given him samples of a new antidepressant.

The medication had certainly helped his "anxiety and blues" as he called it, even though he was being awakened frequently. He hadn't told Sarah; didn't want her to know about the dreams. He didn't really know what they meant, but the last three had been doozies. In the first one he had found himself strolling around the fancy mall in Buckhead. He had only been there in real life a couple of times, accustomed as he was to living in the country. And the retail fare there was way above his tastes and pay grade. But in this dream, he was sprinting across the mezzanine as broken shards of glass rained down upon him. He found himself standing in a storefront, glass display cases shattered and ransacked. He stepped over the limp and bludgeoned body of an elderly man and promptly woke up.

In the second dream he was standing in the middle of the Downtown Connector, the conjoined Interstates 85 and 75 that coursed through the heart of the city. He saw a gasoline tanker snaking, twisting, and pitching over onto its side. A wall of flame erupted from the tanker, engulfing the cab and several cars in its path. A dozen or more vehicles swerved and spun, careening off each other and against the median divider. Again, he awakened before the tanker could crush him.

A third more difficult dream disrupted his equanimity. The vision was as troubling as it was brief. Three young girls lay pale and wet on a riverbank. Their hair was stringy and slippery, caked with mud and strands of algae. Their skin was sallow and blue. A mother's agonized wailing and moaning reached his ears, rising to an eerie crescendo before he roused, sweating and trembling, from his uneasy slumber.

The dreams were certainly frightening. But they became much more terrifying the day he picked up an *Atlanta Journal* from the grocery checkout line.

✻✻✻

Otis had been a firefighter in Atlanta. One day he got trapped and badly burned. He ended up in the big city hospital in the burn unit. He had told Keene, and no one else, about what he had experienced there. Burn therapy is brutal. It requires daily debridement (scrubbing) of the charred and scorched areas to clear these regions of dead tissue that might contribute to infection. Patients are given anesthesia to ease the agony, but the pain is still intense.

Keene had always been one to spend time with his patients. Especially Otis, who had been one of his first patients in his new practice. Keene was always behind schedule but could never say "time's up" to his patients. There was always too much to hear. There was just too much to learn.

Folks in the waiting room who had been with him before consoled those who were first-timers, the ones getting angry and impatient. "Be patient, deary ... he's worth the wait."

Keene collected stories and lives. He couldn't get enough. William Osler, one of the fathers of medicine, famously said: "Listen to your patient ... he's telling you the diagnosis." It was true. Keene, although he had long since abandoned his mystical wanderings, was particularly interested in those stories that were told in hushed tones. The dreams, the supernatural, the spiritual experiences of his patients. And Otis had the most fantastic one of all.

"Doc, you ain't gonna believe this ... but I gotta tell you ..."

"Try me, Otis ... I'm listening."

"You know I'm a Believer, right?"

"Sure, Otis."

"I ain't never told this to nobody until now."

"Go on."

"Well ... when I was in that burn unit. It was hell on earth." Keene had done a rotation in that hospital in med school and knew that unit well. "They took me every day to scrub those burns. Pumped me full of morphine or something to help me out. But it was no good! So, one day I just said to myself, 'Shit! I've had enough,' and I just got up and walked outta there. But then I looked back and there I was, still on that damn table, them working on me. You think I'm crazy, don'tcha?"

Keene listened, transfixed. "No, Otis, I don't think that for a millisecond. Go on."

"Well ... every day after that when they worked on me, I just got up and went for a stroll down the hall. Saw all the docs and nurses, looked at the charts, peeked into other patients' rooms. And just before they got done with my body, I got back in to go back to my room."

*"Did not my spirit go with you?" said the prophet Elisha to his servant, Gehazi, who had gone back to Namaan, the Syrian, whom Elisha had cured of leprosy, surreptitiously seeking the remuneration that Namaan had offered but Elisha had refused. Gehazi was "caught red handed" by the prophet, who had seen the transaction, his having been there "in spirit." And, consequently, the leprosy was put upon the servant* (2 Kings 5).

Out-of-body experience? Astral projection? It was a real human phenomenon described in every culture throughout recorded history. Keene took it all in. He had cared tenderly for this sweet, kind man. Loved him. Prayed with him.

In fact, it was this out-of-body experience that had shown Otis that there was something more to life than this physical world, much more. It led to his becoming a born-again Christian. But the depression Otis had felt had been caving in on him. So, Keene, knowing the connection between the biochemistry of the brain and the outpourings of the soul, tried something, a new drug. It was an antidepressant with the brand name Idyllic, manufactured and newly marketed by Pelzer Pharma. He had met the COO at the gala, the handsome and creepy one, black smoke and everything.

Idyllic had a novel mechanism, so he had read. He understood the neurotransmitters and the reason it might help those who could not pull themselves out of the abyss. He had some in his sample closet. He had given it to Otis months ago. Then, a couple of months later, Otis had come in to see Keene.

"Doc!" Otis's voice had carried an air of panic.

"What's wrong, Otis? Those samples haven't helped?"

"Oh, yeah! They have. I feel a thousand percent better. But there's something else I gotta tell—got to SHOW you. Take a look at this." Otis pulled a worn journal from the backpack he always carried. "Read the last three entries."

The doctor took the little book from Otis's trembling hand. He read:

> *The bodies of three little girls were pulled from the river on the outskirts of the city ... Fiery tanker and twenty-car pileup on the Connector kills eight and injures thirty ... Masked robbers smash up jewelry store in Buckhead mall, killing owner and taking millions in gems ...*

"OK, Otis. So what?" These were huge headline events in Atlanta that had happened last week.

"Doc. Look at the darn dates I wrote those!" he practically screamed. Keene looked down at the journal again. He gasped. The dates of the entries were a week *before* the events.

"Doc, I dreamed these things happening before they happened." The doctor stared vacantly out the window to the grassy park across the street.

"Doc? Say something."

"Huh? Oh, right. Well, Otis, this is certainly a different one for you. I mean, out-of-body is one thing, but pre-cog, um, predicting the future is something else. But honestly, since you're feeling so much better, let's just ride this one out, OK?"

So, they prayed together. Otis went home trembling a bit less. Keene was a bit disconcerted that he hadn't fully addressed his patient's concerns, but, frankly, he was at a loss. Keene retired to his office and brought up the FDA website on his laptop. He registered his observations as a possible adverse

# UNREPORTABLE EVENT

event to the antidepressant "Idyllic" from Pelzer Pharma.

# SALLY (30 A.D.)

Keene continued using and cultivating his special way of engaging, never taking a detached and so-called "objective" approach to patients. They were his friends. In medical school, he had continually been reminded to keep a "professional distance" by his instructors. He was much too personal and transparent for that. He had long ago decided that a personal relationship and self-disclosure were more important than cold objectivity. A clinician was much more likely to come up with a diagnosis and plan of action if they had a more personal connection with the patient. This is what endeared him to his patients and enabled them to open up to him. Another one of these patients was Sally.

"OK, Sally Anderson. You did NOT get these kinds of traumatic injuries as a computer specialist, even if you *were* a Marine." Keene was looking down at papers in a folder she had handed him after she perceived that she was in the presence of a doctor who really cared and listened. She had meticulously documented her medical history. She stated she had been unable to get her full record from the military. "Classified," she explained.

"Look, Doc, I have medical issues. And I've been told you can figure stuff out. So here I am. And, to answer your question, I was part of, shall we say, a very *small* team." Sally was another among the unusual patients in the doctor's practice. That was saying a lot considering the types of patients that came to the doctor and the things they said and did. With Sally Anderson, a willing suspension of disbelief was in order.

Here she was, first visit with the doctor, with a large, organized folder in hand. She was a rather ordinary, somewhat overweight, and unassuming woman in her early fifties. Her blondish Prince Valiant haircut framed a pretty, slightly plump, and boyish face. Her stated occupation was "computer IT specialist," but the medical history read like a combat trauma log. It was.

"Multiple spinal compression fractures. How many times did you skydive?"

"Lost count at three hundred."

"OK. Fractured larynx. How'd you get that?"

"Hand-to-hand combat training mishap. Some ROK soldier got a little overenthusiastic."

"Uh-huh … 'nine-millimeter gunshot wound to the buttocks.' You're pretty darn specific about the type of weapon, aren't you?"

"Gotta know the nature of the beast!"

"So, what happened?"

"Got nailed on exfil. But no worries, my guys took him out before I got on the Blackhawk. They were falling all over themselves to check my wound. A cold day in hell before I showed them MY butt."

"So where did this happen?"

"Some rooftop in, I'll say, uh, Morocco."

"Computer specialist, huh?"

"Yup, my buddies got the hostages, I got the hard drives, just like that."

"Right."

"'AK-47 wound to right upper quadrant with partial liver resection.' Oh, come on, Sally! This is unbelievable!"

"That wasn't in the line of duty, Doc. Ex-husband was DEA. I was walking with him on the way to federal court for him to testify against some cartel gangbanger. Seems he had an amigo who was trying to stop that. Lousy shot. Hit me."

"'Closed head trauma from explosive device.' And this one?"

"Bangkok, US consulate. Protection detail for some fat-cat—and I mean fat—secret diplomat doing some, uh, *negotiations* with God-knows-who. Seems there was a weight-triggered and timed device planted under his limo. Per protocol, we had changed the exit point at the last second, so the driver started the car and moved it to a different location. Fail-safe on the device started a timer just in case the weight sensor didn't work. After the team arrived at the new location, the driver went into the building again. A minute later, *BOOM*. We were seventy-five feet away. Ears are still ringing all the time."

All this and more he saw, poring over her record. Joint aches. GI problems. Muscle pains. Unexplained fatigue, rashes, and on and on.

"That's why I came to you, Doc. None of the other doctors seem to want to take the time to figure me out."

Of course, Keene was all in. He was compelled to figure out this retired Marine Corps master sergeant, IT specialist, and special operator.

"I guess now that you've told me all this, you have to shoot me?" Keene quipped.

"Wouldn't have to," she replied dryly. "'Bout eight ways I could drop you with my bare hands before you got to the door."

Despite her unathletic body habitus, Keene was inclined to believe her. She just grinned ever so slightly.

Over time, Keene peeled back the layers of this fascinating onion, diagnosed some autoimmune issues, and worked with a rheumatologist to help her on the slow road to recovery. They had conversed about her military service, the HALO drops, how she could still task a military satellite from her home computer setup.

"Yeah, but if I did that the phone would ring pretty quick." She shot another sly, subtle grin.

# SCHULTZ (26 A.D.)

Four years earlier, in the executive offices of the Global Financial Council, a sleek steel-and-glass edifice in Brussels, there sat a distinguished-looking gentleman, holding court with members of his inner circle and a couple of representatives of the sycophantic press. He favored the tailored Italian suit, although his frame was decidedly portlier than the skinny and chiseled male models who were featured in the ads.

It was here in this office that the real power in the world lay. All the banks, the government leaders, the old families with their old money, kowtowed to this man. Although he had come up from modest, middle-class means in Germany after the war, he had risen through the European banking and investment community to assume a high place of influence on the world economic scene. While there were hundreds of "financial elites" that regularly held court at well-known rich-boy gatherings such as Davos, there was a much smaller group that exerted control on the European and world money markets. This was a group of no more than a dozen individuals, an exclusive and highly secretive cabal.

These aristocrats, all self-appointed guardians of humanity, knew what was good for the world. They saw that the doomsday clock of global environmental catastrophe was ticking away, and all agreed that something radical had to be done. Hans Schultz was their leading voice, and he articulated for all of them an enlightened, even messianic, vision for leading humanity and saving the planet.

"Gentlemen." He nodded condescendingly. "We all agree, do we not, that mankind is coming to a new era of unprecedented scientific advances? Information technology is progressing exponentially with the development of artificial intelligence."

An eager hand shot up. "Sir, would you tell us more about that?"

"The most exciting developments"—he went on—"are in biological memory storage. Indeed, did you know that DNA is the most efficient place to store masses of information? Did you know AI scientists are now able to program microscopic bits of brain tissue to perform functions that were done with room-sized computers only a few decades ago? We can foresee that, implanted within the human brain, these programmed packets of DNA will become a milestone, nay, a quantum leap that signifies a new age in human evolution. We call it 'transhumanism.'" A group nod ensued from the rapt and worshipful audience of journalists.

"And I might add that the nation that makes the most rapid advances in technology, especially AI, will, frankly, determine and control the New World Order. And while all this may sound frightening to the unenlightened, in fact AI will be used to free mankind from drudgery and toil. And what this really means is that we can utilize the power of AI to develop green technologies, uncover new and innovative sources of energy, and stop the rape of planet Earth. We are all agreed (are we not?) that our fragile sphere cannot sustain the population that we currently have, much less the hordes of consuming, polluting beings that are spawned every minute."

"Sir," one of his aides interjected, "you have a video conference with the German prime minister waiting for you." It was a fabrication on the part of the press secretary, but the soliloquy was getting a tad Hitlerian.

Schultz, founder and president of the Global Financial Council, emerged from sermon mode, brought his focus back, and smiled serenely. "If you'll excuse me, gentlemen." The members of the press dutifully exited the room along with the gentleman's entourage. Two remained behind, one of them the secretary who had spoken of the fictitious video conference. The other was an impossibly handsome man, also in a stylish Italian-cut suit—this one from Saville Row—with exactly the look of the aforementioned Italian models.

"Oh, I do find these little briefings a bit annoying." Schultz sighed.

"Sidney"—he turned to his press secretary—"I don't think I've properly introduced you to Johannes Akhtar, COO of Pelzer Pharmaceuticals. He's just up from Munich for a little tête-à-tête."

The younger man rose politely and nodded in Sidney's direction. "It's a great pleasure to make your acquaintance," Akhtar said smoothly.

"Likewise." Sidney thought to himself that this dashing gentleman did not look like someone who would have a Muslim surname. He was fair skinned with deep, penetrating eyes and a thick head of dark, perfectly coiffed hair. His manicured hands and Jaeger-LeCoultre watch broadcast his expensive tastes and elevated status. Sidney could not help but snatch an up-and-down glimpse of this fellow.

"Aha, Sidney. I know what you're thinking. Mr. Akhtar here is strictly a ladies' man," he said, chortling a bit, "I also know what else you are thinking: 'How could a man who looks like this have the last name of Akhtar?' Well, you see, young Johannes here is the scion of Turkish grandparents who came to Germany after the Great War. They were, shall we say, using an obsolete term, of the *Aryan* race. Thus, the absence of the expected 'swarthiness' of someone from the Middle East." Schultz had drifted in the Hitlerian direction again.

Akhtar nodded again politely, his face inscrutable. He drew a slow, silent breath. The tension that would have appeared in his countenance had been transferred to a tightness in his perfectly toned abs beneath that Italian wool suit. Sidney dismissed himself with a stiff bow. Akhtar and Schultz remained alone. Schultz stood and ambled slowly to the panoramic glass window that looked out upon the city.

Without looking back over his shoulder, he intoned softly, "Am I to understand that we are allies in a certain project? May I offer my assistance at the next phase of your, um, experiment?"

"I'm not sure I get your drift, Mr. Schultz. And how would you do that?"

"I remember every detail of our conversations in New York and in Atlanta. I believe you were there a few years ago for some big gala sponsored by the Emory medical school. You are the COO of the largest and most powerful pharmaceutical company in the world."

"Yes."

"And, as such, you have consolidated your own influence within that world. If I'm not mistaken, you have control over manufacturing as well as distribution of the largest array of medicinal compounds in the world."

"Yes."

"Manufacturing and distribution."

"Your point?" Akhtar scarcely hid his impatience.

"My boy"—Schultz had returned to his chair—"do you think I'm unaware of your travels? Or your ability to procure a variety of, shall we say, raw materials from our friends in the former Soviet Union? Or about your funding of experiments at the medical school in Atlanta and elsewhere? Now, I am acquainted with various, um, parties"—he paused for effect—"who would be able to assist in the manufacture of certain, um, medicines and even help you get them into your supply chain.

"When you are ready, young man, I can help you with bigger and better things."

Akhtar nodded and pushed his chair back. "What makes you think I need your help?"

"Mr. Akhtar, I have already assisted you. Why do you think you had such easy access to the medications that you obtained from Moscow? My friends from the FSB and Stasi made this possible for you. And why do you think your connections to China went so well?"

Akhtar nodded silently and stood to leave.

"Oh, and one more thing," Schultz continued as Akhtar rose, "you are in a position to create a lot of good for the world, and a lot of chaos. To borrow the words of a friend of mine, we should 'never let a good crisis go to waste.'"

As Akhtar exited the room and shut the door, Sidney appeared from behind another paneled entrance, where he had been listening to the conversation.

"He's an extraordinarily clever and capable young man," observed the secretary.

"Indeed," replied Schultz. "And I believe his little *jihad* and my objectives go hand in hand. Let's contact our Chinese friends again. Since our friend Mr. Akhtar has figured out a way to infiltrate the pharma supply, why don't we help him obtain something more effective."

Schultz leaned back in his capacious leather chair and folded his hands in smug satisfaction.

# MAYDAY (33 A.D.)

"Oh, my big feet!" Kaye had laughed as she picked herself up for the second time during their run together one day. But over the next few weeks, her feet, legs, and arms only continued to fail her. They quit laughing.

The sign out front said: Daniel Keene, MD. PHYSICIAN. That sign was mocking him. He felt helpless. He was thirty-three years old and it was still a strange title in his mind. Hard to believe that only a few short years ago he had been a dreamy high school student, wanting to save the world. He still felt like a kid and still looked like one. But now he was a physician with his own general practice. What a circuitous path he had taken to get to this place, wonderful, called, inspired. Now it was terrifying.

His mind was spinning with all that had transpired in the world and in his life.

As those happy days of running with Kaye went along, the "clumsiness" in her feet had kept growing. "I don't know why I've become such a stumble bum lately," she lamented, retrieving Keene's coffee from the kitchen counter. Suddenly and without warning, the mug plummeted to the floor with a smash and splash of latte.

"Honey, what just happened?"

"I don't know. For a second, I just didn't feel it in my hand!"

"OK, that's enough. We're going to see Kaplan today."

He was the neurologist Keene always referred his patients to (when managed care plans allowed it). Kaplan had left his exalted position in academia to finish his career in a private practice, a decision that Keene was ecstatic to hear about when the venerated professor had hung up his shingle near Madison.

The wizened and white-coated doctor finished his touching and probing of Kaye's extremities with a cotton ball, pin, tuning fork, and sundry items. He tested her leg and grip strength.

"You say this started a couple of months ago, and now it seems to be getting worse?"

"Yes, well, I fell down the first time a few years ago. I didn't think anything of it." Kaye's voice trembled a little at the serious expression on the neurologist's face.

"I have a couple of tests to run, some blood tests and a couple of scans."

"Will the scans be a problem, Dr. Kaplan? I'm pregnant!"

"You're what?" Daniel's jaw hit the floor.

"I was going to tell you tonight."

Keene's soul soared and plummeted simultaneously. The best and the worst all at once. Rejoicing at the new life, inwardly despairing at what he suspected the diagnosis to be: ALS.

On the follow-up visit, they got the news.

✧✧✧

"I'm afraid it *is* ALS or something like that," the neurologist opined. Kaplan's expression displayed puzzlement. "I don't really understand completely, I'll have to be honest."

"Yes, and those needles you poked me with in my arms and legs hurt like hell, Ari."

"Sorry, sweetheart. Yes, I know.

"The EMG was relatively normal. I spared you the spinal tap. The MRI of your head, neck, and the rest of your spine was, well, 'normal' but puzzling."

"What do you mean?" inquired Keene.

"Every phase of the scan had a kind of black, smoky haze over it, a little bit like a dark camera lens filter. I've never seen that before. We tried different magnet settings and got the same thing. We thought the machine might be malfunctioning. The repair technician happened to be there; he took off the service panel because he smelled something bad. Even told me he expected to find a dead rodent in there. But nothing was wrong, and it didn't happen with any other patients that day and hasn't since."

Keene startled inwardly for a moment at the mention of smoke and a foul odor. He saw the pasture in his mind's eye, his tornado dreams.

"Nevertheless, your clinical condition, I'm afraid, is progressing exactly the way ALS does, I'm so sorry."

Neither Kaye nor Keene cared for anything but the brutal truth. No mincing of words for them.

Over the course of the second trimester, as Kaye's legs were failing her and her general weakness grew more profound, Keene struggled for answers in his soul. He touched her and prayed for her, hoping against hope to be able to draw this terrible disease out of her.

"Sweetheart," she said soothingly, "you know I'm going to be OK, don't you? In this life or the next? But I want us to have this baby."

Keene could not suppress the sob that erupted from his chest.

A couple of Keene's OB/GYN friends made special arrangements to come to the carriage house to conduct the prenatal visits. They even managed to bring over an ultrasound to track the baby's progress.

"She's doing just fine," they agreed.

But Keene was finding it difficult to function in life and in his practice. Without telling anyone of the crushing anxiety and fear he was experiencing, he decided to self-medicate. From the sample closet, he retrieved some of the Idyllic he had given to Otis. Despite the weird effects it had had on the firefighter initially, he had done well for a couple of years and it had proven marvelously effective up to this point in snatching him back from the pit of despair. Otis had made no mention of any more recurring predictive dreams.

But still, curiously, Keene pondered that he had never heard back from the FDA. The "reportable event" system was supposed to support rapid closed-loop communication. But now, for himself, he had to do something to keep going.

Now here they were, nearly seven months into her pregnancy. Kaye was scarcely able to move, and a machine now assisted her breath, a mask over her face at night. And sometimes all day as well.

"Daniel, my darling ... we're going to have this baby. Save our child, my sweet. I love you so much."

# CRASHING (33 A.D.)

Keene gently and quietly closed the door to the carriage house and tried to play hopscotch along the slate path that ran under the wisteria-draped arched trellis to the back of his office. He hoped a little play would help his sinking soul. It didn't work. Something else did though, a little.

"No! Get down, Tigger. No! No! I can't play right now!"

He was hissing at that whirling dervish of a dog: Tigger, the boxer. The only possible name for a brindle, tiger-striped dog that spent more time in orbit than on solid ground. Bouncy and as much a puppy at the age of five as she had been at five months. He and Kaye had acquired her when they first moved into the house and office five years earlier. Despite her unruliness, her zeal for her master did help his mood a bit.

Tigger knew she was not allowed to jump on a person in her enthusiasm. Keene's firm, forceful, yet gentle hand had trained her well in her puppyhood. No doubt she was thinking: "But I want to love you to death, to jump all over you and cover you with doggy kisses. I know, I know, I know … I'll just have to settle for spinning back flips all around you, and maybe you'll play with me, please, please, PLEASE!"

Keene pushed past the animated animal, resolute along his path. The fragrance of gardenias flooded his senses, lending all the more to the angst that threatened his equanimity, an anxiety that now grew daily.

Gardenias. Smell and memory. Nary a thought between the fragrance and the recall, the past event, the experience, sight, smell, sound, whole body. Hippocampus and olfactory lobe.

"You can't just reduce everything in the observable empirical world to a mechanistic sequence of 'causes and effects,'" Keene would often say to med students or residents under his tutelage, or to patients who were seeking answers.

Created in the image of God? Why is the olfactory lobe right next to the seat of memory? Why is the perfume industry so big? Why do you take a whiff of those cinnamon buns and immediately you're in your grandma's kitchen? God Himself "smelled the smoke" of the burnt offering, saw the rainbow, *remembered* His covenant with his people (Gen 8 and 9).

"It makes perfect theological and biological sense, y'know? That our physical bodies should be the material manifestation, the worldly image of the Godhead. After all, this 'temple of flesh' was created to house the Spirit of God Himself." This was a frequent closing statement that he offered to his students or anyone who showed enough interest to listen.

And he knew what to expect from his true love's diagnosis. He'd already helped others over the threshold, holding their hands and the hands of their loved ones and praying. Why did this happen to Kaye? The world, life, was going so perfectly. Keene trusted in the sovereignty of God; all things happen for a purpose, according to His plan. How could this possibly be part of His plan?

And where was the healing energy that he knew and had experienced with so many others? At night while Kaye slept, he prayed fervently, laying hopeful hands upon her slumbering form, waiting for the light, the heat of healing to course through him and into her. It never came.

"Hi, Annie!" He tried his best to be cheerful as he burst through the back door of his office.

"Hi, Doc," was the casual reply. "How's our girl today?"

"About the same ... had a pretty good night ... pulse ox was fine. She's comfortable."

"That's good. I'm praying night and day."

Keene thought back on his first encounters with his office manager. Annie was a gem. A diminutive powerhouse and a firecracker of a woman, all four feet ten of her. A preacher's wife. Twice. Twice widowed. First husband was a preacher who died behind the wheel. He had been an over-the-road trucker and a real tentmaker preacher. He had fallen asleep from exhaustion. Second husband, also a retired preacher, died of lung cancer. She was a rock.

They had met the first time Keene had made rounds in the hospital. She was the unit clerk. A friendship had sparked between the two of them.

"Hey, Doc?" she had asked.

"Yeah?"

"I've heard you're opening up your office ... soon?"

"Sure will."

"Ya think you're gonna need a manager?"

And that was it. She was everything that he could have hoped for. Kind. Efficient. Organized (preacher's wife). Above all, she was caring, the perfect extension of his own heart. And she loved Kaye. Kaye loved her back.

"Doc, I need to talk to you." Annie sounded urgent as Keene entered the back door. He saw the troubled look on her face.

"Sure."

Keene and Annie stepped into his office while patients drifted into the waiting room and lined up at the locally crafted front desk to sign in. The office was starting to hum with activity.

"I don't know how to say this any other way, Doc. I got word that Otis took his life last night. Shot himself in the head."

"Oh my God!" Otis, the brave and mysterious firefighter, was dead. What had happened? He had seemed to be doing so well.

But now Keene felt so responsible. It was he who had given those samples to his patient. The samples had worked. And then they hadn't.

But there was another thing: the depression Otis had felt had been caving in on the doctor as well.

How do you cope when your whole world comes crashing down around you? Keene had had it all: a calling fulfilled; a beautiful, athletic, and loving wife; a good name; a growing reputation in the community. Now it was falling apart. His wife was dying. The new life inside her hung in the balance. He couldn't sleep. Concentrating was difficult. He felt unable to maintain his usual state of cozy calmness.

The pills worked. His mood, concentration, and sleep improved. He could function. But then his own nightmares had come. The same dream almost every night. And they weren't about tornados. Each night a horrific narrative progressed a little further. What was this recurring nocturnal vision? Could it *really* be that he was seeing something that was yet to happen, just as Otis had reported to him? He did not know.

# THE JOURNAL (33 A.D.)

The police chief tipped his hat somberly and nodded at the doctor as he exited Otis's house. "So sorry, Doc. Otis was a good man. I know you guys was close. Heck, Doc, you're close with all of us."

Chief Tumbleston was Keene's patient, too. And, yes, he felt close to the doctor as everyone else who came under his care did.

"Thanks, Chief. Is she ready to see me?"

"Of course. We're all done here. You'll sign the death certificate, right?"

"Sure."

The mortuary van was just pulling away. He let himself in the front door. Keene held Otis's aging wife, Sarah, in a weeping embrace. She seemed a decade older now, crumbling. No words would do here. Just touch. One of those times that there's nothing else to be done except hold someone close, or just hold their hand.

Sarah was a portly woman who usually smothered her company with the radiant embrace of a warm, smiling, rosy face and lively round eyes. Now she was pale, pinched, seemingly having lost all the loving fullness of her countenance. Her eyes were empty, red-rimmed, puffy.

"Doc," she finally whispered. "I didn't show the chief this." She pulled the worn-out journal from the front pocket of her apron.

"Yeah, he showed me too."

"That was a couple of years ago, Doc. I think—I think I know why he did it."

"Why?"

"Doc. Lately Otis had been talking, well, *crazy!* He was staying up night after night, pacing around and talking to himself. He was writing like mad all the time in this journal." She gestured toward Keene with the journal, then pulled it back close to the fresh apron she wore. Keene spied a spot of crimson on her blouse that the apron failed to cover completely.

"He kept saying, 'It's just too much, everywhere, everywhere,' and he'd write something else down in this book. He was frantic and out of his mind, Doc. I was going to call you this morning to get him in to see you.

"Last night when I couldn't stay awake anymore, he was pacing around upstairs and down, and he kept saying over and over, 'Gotta make it stop, gotta make it stop.' Then I heard the last thing that he said before I went to sleep. I—I just couldn't stay awake anymore to watch him." Her voice trailed off. She stifled a sob. "I should have taken him to Emergency right then. It was the last thing he said. The last thing he said was, 'Gotta make it stop. I know how to make it stop.'"

"What are you thinking, Sarah?"

"I think he really ... *crazy, crazy* ... really thought that if he was gone, stuff wouldn't happen?" She paused at the statement, the half question. Her mournful look of regret obliterated her otherwise kind and gentle countenance as she handed the journal to the doctor.

"Read the last entry, Doc."

Keene took the journal from her trembling hand and quickly flipped the pages. He caught a glimpse of what now seemed to be hundreds of entries, each more hastily and frantically scribbled than the ones previous. He noted that, instead of brief, infrequent prophetic notes of local and regional bad news, there were notes on events both near and remote. From Madison to Minneapolis to Mexico. Furthermore, the follow-up notes he scribbled after the bad events noting the dates they happened were all over the place. Some predictions predated the events by a couple of days, some by weeks, and some had yet to transpire. Then there was the last entry:

> *Doctor and invalid pregnant wife found murdered in historic suburban town of Madison, Georgia. Assailant or assailants unknown. Office ransacked. Police searching for clues, motives.*

# FBI (33 A.D.)

In the days after raiding the sample closet and in the following weeks he had been taking the same Idyllic that he had given to Otis, Keene had indeed felt better, despite the dreams. Up to that point, as far as Keene had known, Otis had seemed on the outside to be okay. Other than hinting at a few disturbing things that were occurring in his imagination, and a few dreams that he hadn't yet shared, Otis had seemed, by all rights, to be much better, until this. And now the doctor carried a burden that was impossible to bear: Otis's death and the last prophecy.

Upstairs in the carriage house, his love continued to drift inexorably away. The once athletic, cocky, vivacious Kaye was confined now to a hospital bed. Barely able to move. Requiring total assistance for nearly everything. And as her life slowly went away, she carried that other life along and away inside her. Keene felt his own life ebbing as well.

He often wept silently, head on the bedspread at her side as she slept. "Lord, Jesus, heal her, or else don't make her suffer anymore, and just TAKE her; but don't take our child, too." It was a race against time.

"There's nothing we can do," the neurologist reiterated what several of his colleagues had already said. "We can just pray that this baby gets far enough along before …" His voice faltered as he looked on the young doctor's ashen face.

And now Keene's own dreams began to turn even more bizarre and chaotic. They replayed the same scene over and over. Each night it would unfold a little at a time: Violent. Explosions. Glass shattering. He was at the center, running and getting nowhere, legs like molasses, the entrance to the carriage house looming before him, and the stairs to his beloved. But he could not ever get there. Amid it all was a smoky, black, foul, evil shadow.

Now the doctor revisited a thought that increased his frightful burden exponentially:

"As much as this antidepressant sample helped Otis and me, there can be no doubt that something bad is in it, a hallucinogenic agent, and now I'm seeing the future, too?"

✯✯✯

Two years earlier, after his initial attempt to report Otis's dreams, Keene had pulled up the FDA Adverse Events Reporting System, or FAERS, website once again and clicked away on the form. Per the instructions, he had followed his first report multiple times. He had tried an FOIA request to confirm that the reportable event was registered in their database. Nothing. No evidence that the report had gone through. He had emailed the pharma company (Pelzer, Manhattan HQ) to inquire. Nothing. It seemed like a dead end to Keene. He was about willing to seek out any source of assistance. One particular avenue of inquiry involving a retired professor from the University of Georgia ended up even more disturbing.

"Hello, Doctor."

"Hi, Professor Alfonzo." The doctor rested his gaze upon a skinny, hunched man with a wise, troubled face that, despite its careworn demeanor, failed to hide a pair of twinkling eyes that broadcast warmth and humor. "So, you teach at Georgia?"

"It's what I'm doing in retirement. I teach a class on Death and Dying. You know, Elisabeth Kübler-Ross stuff. Young people really need to hear these things. It's what I love to do."

"What did you do before?"

"For most of my adult life," the professor replied with a distinct Italian accent, "I was with the Italian Secret Service. I worked in counterintelligence with the CIA, MI6, and others. My field was bioterrorism."

"Wow. It says here that you don't really have anything medical to discuss today."

"No. Just getting established. You are acquiring quite a reputation around here, young man."

"Thank you." Keene was now officially bursting with anticipation. "Well, if you don't really have anything medical to discuss with me, I've actually got something I want to share with you. You see, I'm, uh, writing a book," Keene lied. "And I wonder if this situation is plausible: The main character, a doctor, suspects that certain prescription drugs in his sample supply have been contaminated by someone in the supply chain, with, like, a hallucinogen or something. You know, a modern-day poisoned Tylenol scare, like what happened in the eighties."

The professor looked at Keene intently. As a former spy accustomed to interrogations, he knew when someone was lying. He leaned in closer to the doctor, who sat on a high stool beside the exam table. His glasses slid down toward the end of his Roman nose. He peered over the lenses, stared deeply into the doctor's eyes in a most penetrating fashion, and inquired quite seriously, "Son, how much do you already know about what I used to do?"

✯✯✯

Keene, ever the researcher, scoured all the medication and pharma and government websites he could find. He had continued to give Otis samples over the following couple of years to save Otis money. They were the same samples Keene now took for himself. He looked for any evidence that contaminated sample containers of Idyllic had been found or suspected. Nothing. He looked to see if any reports of any kind on this medication had surfaced now that it had been in general sales for a couple of years. Nothing. Could the contaminated samples just be an isolated event? He had one more place to check.

Oriole Health Distribution Center was only about five miles from his little town. A lot of folks he knew and took care of worked there. He called in a favor.

"What did you want to look at, Doc?" inquired Frank, one of his patients who had grown progressively more curious. He was chief of the pharma distribution warehouse's security and had let Keene into the facility after hours that day.

"I'm looking for shipments from Pelzer Pharm. Specifically this new antidepressant, Idyllic."

"Oh, yeah, I heard about that one. Supposed to be really good for people who are down in the dumps. It's bein' advertised a lot. Yeah. Yeah … it's right over here. See? There are the bigger pallets that'll be broken up and shipped to the pharmacies. And over here, you see, are smaller pallets that get broken down and given to the local sales teams through another distribution center, although they are going almost completely now to drop-shipping the samples and the reps hardly ever touch 'em."

Keene recognized the Pelzer logo on all the shrink-wrapped cargo. Something immediately caught his eye. The style and color of the wrapping was different on one of the smaller sample pallets. The strapping tape was different as well. Just one of them. It had the usual barcode markings that helped track inventory and security. But it just looked different.

"Are all these drugs shipped from the same facility?"

"As far as I know. Mexico, I think."

"Not China?"

"Nope, Pelzer don't make stuff there."

"Then why are there Chinese characters along the edge of this pallet?" Sure enough, adjacent to the bar codes was a row of Chinese writing. He pondered the discovery on the way home.

China. Again. They were very skilled at ripping off Western technology, electronics, patented chemical compounds, pharmaceuticals, you name it. Could these samples be intended to become a biological weapon? Could they be planning on putting something else into the pharma supply chain? How could he get someone in federal law enforcement to check this out? His mind raced uneasily as he slipped into the recliner beside Kaye's bed that night. Something was not right here. He knew he would have more of that nightmare tonight.

The next morning, he called the FBI office in the city and asked for the special agent in charge. He tried not to sound as unbalanced as he felt while voicing his sketchy theory to the agent. The agent didn't sound at all impressed. Keene knew he was being blown off. Or maybe he was just paranoid. By now Keene was speculating that something much worse than adulterated samples was afoot. What he was thinking froze his already frayed nerves and sent an uncontrollable shudder up and down his spine: bioweapons, viruses.

He expounded on the terrifying theory; the Western world had just been rocked by a viral pandemic that had purportedly incubated in bats in the wild near a Chinese city. But DNA sequencing of the virus showed clearly that it had been genetically engineered. It had "escaped" from a Chinese viral research facility.

"Agent Ward, you're not listening to me. I told you that I reported the antidepressant samples to the FDA. I know the effects they caused. The FAERS system didn't report back to me. I tried multiple times."

"Must have been a glitch," was the response.

"Look, Agent Ward, I tried over and over. Got no answer. What if someone at Pelzer can do something to that vaccine they've got on the shelf?"

"OK, Doc. I'll look into it."

✫✫✫

This virus had wreaked havoc. But the fear that descended upon the world caused even more damage, as entire economies were locked down, children were forced out of school, families were disrupted, and small businesses were driven entirely out of business. The fear was stoked by inflated death statistics and daily pronouncements by the experts giving somber and often contradictory advice on how not to get infected or infect others.

The medical community on the front lines overreacted most of all. Fear stalked the corridors of medical centers and clinics, and draconian quarantine methods only made isolation worse and contributed to increased death and damage from other causes besides the virus. Pelzer Pharm, among others, had profited immensely, having developed one of the main vaccines, as well as a drug to combat the spread. The pharma industry contributed, along with government agencies and self-important officials, to a campaign of information suppression that rivaled book burnings in other times and other places on Earth.

Brave doctors who dared to question the wisdom of Big Medicine, Big Academia, Big Pharma, and Big Government were stripped of their academic appointments. In some cases, doctors lost their licenses for spreading "misinformation" despite strong worldwide data indicating there were effective and cheap medications that could treat the virus. On top of that, data in possession of the CDC early in the worldwide vaccination campaign showed clearly that the "jab" being touted as the best protection from the virus was actually a source of considerable misery and death. It took nearly a year and a half of legal maneuvers and lawsuits to force the CDC to release this information that would have taken hours to put out to the public early on.

What is Truth? Pelzer Pharm and others had strong incentive to suppress the truth. Hundreds of billions of dollars were at stake, riding on a clause in the Emergency Use Authorization Act handed down by the government. That clause states that to be authorized for emergency use in such a rapid fashion, there can be no other effective treatment. No wonder the entirety of pharma, academia, Big Medicine, Big Tech platforms, and Big Government (the FDA, CDC, and every other federal institution) were in lockstep on this. They systematically suppressed, ridiculed, and oppressed all those "purveyors of misinformation" who were, in fact, just stating the facts. Even though the FDA had retracted its previous pejorative statements about Ivermectin, the official position—based upon skewed investigations and faulty research design—was that Ivermectin was "ineffective" against COVID. There was way too much money involved. Everyone had their fingers in the pie except the ones who were trying to tell the truth.

Now, even though the scourge of the pandemic was over, fear persisted. People still wore masks in public places. Some even wore them in their cars, or even when walking or jogging in solitude. And people in shops, stores, and libraries still unconsciously and reflexively practiced social distancing, an oxymoron if ever there was one, he thought.

Keene saw this pharmaceutical company in the middle of the COVID pandemic. And it was now poised to be at the epicenter of the next pandemic, a pandemic that had yet to happen, a virus that wasn't even on the radar yet. The "experts" had been predicting this since before COVID. Pelzer had now developed a new "one size fits all" vaccine, purported to be effective against nearly all viruses. Fear, the prime motivator still, had a hundred million Americans already signed up. They had made their reservations for the jab as soon as it came out. The doses were standing by, ready. The lemmings were lined up to jump off the cliff.

Wasn't this the ideal opportunity for a well-placed and widely scattered contamination of, say, just a hundred thousand of the hundred million doses with a really dangerous virus bioengineered in a Chinese lab? Hadn't virus researchers in Canada years before already shipped several deadly viruses to that Chinese lab, ostensibly in the name of pure scientific research and "for the good of humanity?" This was the theory that Keene had spun to the special agent in charge. But the agent had ended the conversation, politely but abruptly, with an empty promise.

It was only two days after this conversation with the agent that the vehicle began showing up, the cliché classic black SUV with tinted windows. It loitered across the street next to the grassy park, or on the side streets, or in the alley, or cruised slowly around the small town.

"What is going on here?" Keene directed his query at the chief of police, who sat in the empty waiting area at lunchtime polishing off the last of what had been several large doughnuts a drug rep had brought that morning.

"Hell if I know, Doc. They ain't doin' nothin' illegal. They're scouting properties, they said. And mostly they just sit in their car and talk and eat."

"Well, could you run their tag or something?"

"I'll do that when I get back to the office. Darn computer in my car is broke."

"Okay."

✯✯✯

"Hey, Doc, I ran the tag," said the chief over the telephone later. "Car belongs to some real estate investment company, just like the guys said. It's up in Virginia, in Langley."

# DESPAIR (33 A.D.)

"Good morning, Julie." Keene greeted the hired caregiver as she entered and he exited the carriage house. "She had a good night. Everything is all set up. Call me if you need to."

Julie smiled sweetly and patted the doctor on the shoulder. "I got this, y'know?"

He gently and quietly closed the door to the carriage house and tried again to play hopscotch along the slate path in hopes that it might elevate his sinking soul, but to no avail.

"No! Get down, Tigger. No! No! I STILL can't play right now!"

The dervish dog did not relent. Still spun in circles but never touched Keene. "Shadow boxer," he thought, zigzagging along, taking evasive maneuvers. Despite his general downcast demeanor, he still found this dog to be a lifter of spirits even now. This was the pup who had been an all-too-frequent interloper on their lovemaking over the years if they forgot to close the door. He ached for that opportunity that would never come again.

He continued the hopeless hopscotch. The fragrant floral scents tormented him all the way. As he was about to enter the back door of the office, he heard the squeak of the gate behind him and a voice cried out, "Hey, Doc." It was Fred.

"Fred!" Keene was shocked and amazed. "I thought you were gone for good after they fired you at Emory. I didn't know where you went."

"Well, Doc," Fred replied in a conspiratorial tone, "I kind of had to go underground for a while. Not only did Emory and those clinical researchers want a piece of my hide, but the folks that run me out of town where I was trying to preach before were after me too. But I found you. You're doing good, Doc. But I know Kaye isn't."

"No," Keene stammered and choked back a sob. "She isn't. And there's a lot of other stuff going on that's scary and hard to explain." Keene proceeded breathlessly to explain (with the *Reader's Digest* version) the strange events of the past months and weeks. "But all that pharmaceutical stuff is not as important as Kaye. Will you come up with me to see her?"

"You DO know that's why I came today," Fred stated ever so kindly. Fred followed Keene up the stairs in the carriage house to the bedroom where Kaye lay. The ventilator was whirring and hissing. Julie was tending to Kaye with a cleansing wipe.

"I'm back. Jules, this is Fred. Fred, Jules." Turning to Fred, he said, "Jules has been a lifesaver, tending to my sweetheart." Kaye nodded in agreement as enthusiastically as she could. A broad smile appeared beneath the mask over her face.

Competing with the alternating air pressure that the device was applying over her nose and mouth, she let out a muffled greeting to Fred. "Oh, Fred! Good to see you. You disappeared!"

"Yup. But I'm back, Kaye. I'd sure like to help. May I?"

Kaye nodded. Julie stood back against the wall and watched attentively. She had heard Keene talk about Fred and his healings. Was she about to witness one? Fred stood next to Kaye's bed and leaned forward, placing his hands over her sternum and upper abdomen, closing his eyes in silent contemplation. For what seemed like an eternity, nothing whatsoever happened. It was a frozen moment in time, full of expectation on behalf of all present, especially Keene. The only thing breaking the silence was the mechanical sighing of the breath-assist device and the jiggling and sloshing of the connecting tubing that pooled water as it conducted the oxygenated air under pressure to her mask.

Abruptly and without warning, Fred staggered back and did an ungraceful butt-plant on the floor. He stared blankly ahead, uttering not a sound. "This is where," Keene whispered to Julie, "Fred takes whatever is ailing his patient into himself and then gets rid of it." He had explained this phenomenon to Julie, having witnessed it in the units of Emory on several occasions.

But no such thing happened. Fred continued to sit, looking stunned. A familiar foreboding seemed to sweep over Keene, the same feeling he had experienced on the night he had taken Kaye to see the healer, and again at the gala as he looked over at the pain doctors deep in conversation with Mr. Akhtar of Pelzer Pharma.

Then he saw it, sensed it: what appeared to be a thin black veil of smoke wafting around and across Kaye and vacillating in a purposeful rhythm like a tug-of-war between Kaye and Fred. He half expected to smell the ozone of a shorted-out electrical wire on the BiPAP machine, but no sensation reached his nostrils or any other of his senses except a prickly, crawling heat that traversed his spine and the back of his neck. Then, suddenly, the odor of burning flesh infiltrated his nose. He was seized with terror, the same fear he had felt long before looking out over that cow pasture and smelling that awful fire.

Suddenly, the dark blanket rose and detached itself from the space around Fred. Then it spread across Kaye, descending like a shroud, and disappeared.

"What just happened?" inquired Julie hesitantly after an eternal minute.

"I don't know. Fred ... Fred!"

Kaye looked to be in a deep slumber. For her it was not a reassuring look.

"Fred!"

Fred aroused and shook his head briskly as if trying to rid his hair of a pesky bug. He stood up, looked down at the sleeping Kaye, then over at Julie, and said calmly, "She's gonna be okay. Doc, you were headed over to see patients when I caught you. Let me walk with you over there."

They said their goodbyes to Julie and proceeded down the stairs and out the carriage house door toward the office.

"Doc, sorry for the quick exit but I had to get you out here to explain. There's something else going on here. I didn't take anything out of her, at least not anything like any physical disease. Whatever is ailing her, it's not of flesh and blood. It's dark. And it's at war with her, probably cause of you. It's at war with me, too, ever since I tried to preach the Gospel in my own town." Fred's demeanor carried a sense of urgency, as a man on an emergency mission. "Listen, Doc, I gotta go check on something, but I'll be back tomorrow, okay?"

"Sure, Fred. Maybe then you can explain better what's going on?"

"I hope so. Doc, did you smell something?" he asked. Without waiting for an answer as he departed hastily through the gate.

Keene entered the back door of the mansion office; he greeted his staff once more in as cheerful a manner as he could muster. He was struggling not to run back up to Kaye's bedside, but he knew Julie would inform him quickly if anything untoward were to happen.

"Doc," said Annie, "first patient is Sally."

Keene and Sally had continued their rapport, bolstered no doubt by her gratitude to him for being the first one to finally listen and help her make progress in her healing. So, at the opportune moment, the doctor spilled his guts and all his terror right there in the exam room.

"Sally, if you don't mind, today is gonna be about me."

"What's wrong, Doc?" She knew fear when she encountered it. She had been there, done that a lot, personally and professionally.

"I think something terrible is going on, and something's about to happen. And I don't know what to do about it. I need—I need help. And I don't know where to turn." He then proceeded to tell the former marine special operator the whole story: how he had seen and experienced the effects of a tainted antidepressant; how he had reported the adverse events to the FDA and to the pharmaceutical company itself.

He told her he had never received a response or acknowledgment from anyone and had been unable to see if his query was ever received or registered in the government system. He told her about finding the pallet of the antidepressant samples in the drug distribution warehouse. How he knew that there was a Chinese connection between counterfeit manufacturers and Pelzer Pharma. Then he explained his deeper fear: If someone in the pharma supply chain could do this, what if something bigger were at play?

Keene explained his skepticism of the pharma industry and its profit motive, how he had watched the hysteria over the recent worldwide viral pandemic, and the rush to manufacture and distribute a vaccine to stem the tide of the disease. Apart from the obvious failures of the recent push to vaccinate the whole world, Keene expounded upon his terrifying hypothesis: that another yet-to-be-identified but approaching viral pandemic was going to drive over a hundred million patients in the US to jump on the next vaccine bandwagon.

He knew that the vaccine was ready to go and Pelzer was at the center of it all. If someone in Pelzer could slip hallucinogens manufactured in China into the supply chain, what if they could do something to the vaccine supply? He trembled as he spoke. Furthermore, he related his conversation with John Ward, the SAIC of the Atlanta FBI office. He felt totally blown off by the guy after having told him the exact story he spun now to Sally.

"What was that name again?" she asked. Sally was ordinarily as inscrutable as the Sphinx; her marine stoicism had molded her demeanor into a mostly monotone poker face. But her eyes darted sideways a bit.

"Yes! And there's more. After I talked to that jerk, that's when that government-looking SUV started prowling around the town. I found out they are registered with some real estate company. In Langley freakin' Virginia? Oh, yeah, right.

"Sally, my wife is dying, and now I think I've taken the lid off Pandora's box. I've stuck my nose into some place I was never meant to go. But there it is. I'm really afraid." His voice faltered. He stifled a sob as hot tears burnt his cheeks. Sally put a hand on the doctor's trembling shoulder.

"Hey, Doc. Look, um, I may know some people."

✪✪✪

"Mr. Akhtar, sir?" A burly and rather obsequious man in a business suit, with a bulge at the armpit, nudged open the door to Johannes's corner office, which presided over the Manhattan skyline. "Thought you ought to know …"

"Yes?"

"I don't know what this means, but it was our guy at Justice on the phone about 'that nosy doctor in Georgia' … And said you should be told about it."

"Thank you."

The bodyguard left and Johannes reached for his cellphone, the burner. The conversation was brief. Akhtar nodded solemnly as he listened to the authoritarian voice on the other end of the line.

"Yes, I have been made aware of this situation." He spoke quietly and slowly. "I have received a few reports from other locations but they have been few and far between. But this particular doctor is being quite persistent. He has been breaking down the doors at the FDA as well as with FAERS reports. Oddly enough, I think I know this doctor. I met him in the company of two of our associates at the Emory gala." He paused a moment to listen. He took a deep breath.

"Yes, as close as we are to the goal, I think it behooves us to control this situation once and for all … Yes, I understand."

The commanding voice on the line responded, "Quickly now. See what he has then. And finish it."

Akhtar clicked off the phone grimly.

# FLASHPOINT (33 A.D.)

"How'd she do today, Julie?" enquired Keene the next afternoon.

"She kinda had a hard time, Doc. She's acting just like she did when she heard about Otis a few weeks ago. She's flagging a bit more since Fred was here. Seems like faster than before. And I had to put the BiPAP mask on her a bit longer today. She was a bit short of breath. But she ate some soup for supper. I got her cleaned up and she's asleep. I think she's pretty stressed, your being at work pretty much all day and all. I knew you'd need to see her again tonight. Well, anyway, I think she's comfortable and she'll probably sleep all night. I'll say g'night then."

"Thanks, Jules. You ARE a jewel! I wonder why Fred didn't come back today?"

Keene patted the nurse on the shoulder affectionately as she made her way out of the door and into the courtyard, having kept the long day's vigil. It was later than usual, nine o'clock and getting dark. He trudged wearily up the stairs to the bedroom, practically tripping over the stair lift he'd had installed when Kaye had more mobility but became too weak to make the climb.

"Won't have any use for that pretty soon," he thought to himself in morbid, mournful resignation. "Don't you dare think like that!" He took to castigating himself for putting up the white flag. Still, as he crept quietly into the darkened room, it was difficult to keep his composure.

There his darling lay. Her arms rested on the soft feather pillows he had bought her. The pillows reminded him of happier times, of their "honeymoon" that had been delayed a few years after med school by poverty and the necessity of finishing training.

The pillowcases and linen on the bed rocked a romantic Italian scene of Tuscany, with rolling hills under a pink sunset. She loved it so, and being surrounded by it, she was at least able to be transported in her dreams to a better place.

At the foot of the hospital bed hung a hopeful pair of pink and green spangled running shoes, dangling in the dim light expectantly, wishing to be filled again by those feet that once pranced but were now thin and beginning to look shriveled. Keene's own shoes hung nearby. The hook by the door remained empty. The compact respirator hummed on the bedside stand, and Kaye's chest rose and fell with the clicking rhythm of the machine. It was difficult to discern whether she was exerting the effort to breathe or if it was the device. Either way, she did look comfortable, and her pulse oxygen monitor showed good numbers.

He wanted to kiss her forehead and caress her blond locks, but he didn't want to wake her. He gently ran his hand over the protuberant belly, resting it ever so slightly over her navel. He felt the reassuring tumble of the sleeping child within who, upon his touch, obediently assumed another position with a slosh and a little kick, as if to reassure the young doctor, "I'm okay, Dad." He sighed deeply, sucking in the cool air of relief and resignation, and sat down.

Sinking into the recliner chair beside the bed where he had slept these last few months, he was too exhausted even to wash his face and don his pajamas. He drifted off into a fitful doze, the kind of half-sleep, half-wake state with which he was so familiar. It was the "one eye open" kind of non-rest that he had learned to do so well in residency, keeping watch over critical care patients in the ICU from the darkened call room next door to the unit. The sound of Kaye's machine only served to heighten the sense of déjà vu.

He hadn't slept … or had he? "It's more silent than it ought to be," he thought, an eerie disquietude flooding his slowly rising awareness of the surroundings. A muffled yelp from the courtyard jerked him to attention.

"Tigger? What the heck? What's she doing out?" He peered through the darkened room to the dim glow of the wall clock. Two o'clock. Tigger was ordinarily put up for the night in a utility room at the back of the main house and office. They moved her accommodations to that location some months ago when her rambunctious affection became too much for Kaye and her caregivers to put up with in the carriage house.

"Guess the door got left unlatched." Keene swayed a bit as his feet gained purchase on the carpeted floor. He sighed deeply and steeled his will to retrieve the wayward pup from the courtyard, put her away, and see if he could get back to the chair and obtain a reasonable night's rest. He hadn't even taken his shoes off. But as he exited the carriage house and stepped onto the slate path, a deep foreboding overcame him. Something was terribly wrong.

# UNREPORTABLE EVENT

The muggy late-summer night was stifling as usual. But the familiar droning buzz of the cicadas in the trees was eerily silent. And the small motion-activated light at the back of the office that would have been illuminating the area upon Keene's entry (or Tigger's bouncing) was dark. Keene pulled his cellphone from his back pocket. He'd been too tired even to empty them before drifting off in the recliner. The meager flashlight provided enough illumination for him to make his way toward the back of the office and to the utility shed where Tigger was supposed to be asleep.

He tiptoed carefully in the dim light to gain a better view. Tigger would have been barking loudly if there had been an intruder and she had been loose. There was no sign of her. Then he saw her. At his feet below the back porch of the main office lay a dark lump. The top of the lump rose and fell erratically, and a faint gurgling and whistling sound accompanied each movement. It was Tigger. Keene quickly stooped to touch the furry mound, only to draw back a wet hand, the warmth and aroma of which conveyed in an instant that this was blood and that Tigger was near death.

He had not one millisecond to process the finding or to render care. A dim reflection and flash of light coming from inside the office bounced off the broken pane of the back door. He heard the hollow, metallic rending of file cabinet drawers.

"Lord Jesus! They're here!"

An invisible hand constricted his throat, and his chest pounded out an awful, panicked cadence. Keene recognized that hyperventilation was not too far away. He summoned his years of competitive endurance training to calm his breath, slow his heart rate, and steady his nerves. He stooped down as low as his trembling legs would let him and crawled and duck-walked as quickly as he could back down the flagstones to the carriage house.

"Got to get to Kaye. Oh, Jesus, oh, God, it's happening for real now."

He misjudged the first step and his knee descended with a soft percussion on the bottom plank.

From the darkness behind, he heard voices half aloud, half whispered, urgent and ominous. Several soft reports and low flashes behind him coincided with an eruption of splintered wood from the carriage house porch that stung his cheeks and neck. He also felt and heard a wet thump in the back of his left shoulder, followed by a searing heat. "Shot for the first time," he realized as the thought streaked through his racing brain.

Straining to see through the closed screen door from the porch into the entry hall, he spied the dark outline of a skulking man rounding the antique banister and beginning to head up the stairs. As much to escape the doom that closed in behind him as to intercept the figure by any means possible, he leapt to his feet and crashed straight through the screen door, separating the door from its hinges and bringing half the frame crashing inward. Door, screen, and man careened across the short stretch of foyer. Keene sprawled face down onto the foot of the stairs as flashes, splinters, and shattered glass rained down. He felt a warm stream of liquid above his ear. It stung.

Keene's forward momentum had plunged him through the door and barreled him into the back of the startled intruder, sending them both headlong onto the foot of the stairs. The intruder rolled over and struggled to get up and rid himself of the angry body on top of him. He slung his close combat automatic rifle around swiftly, striking Keene across the cheek.

Keene, momentarily stunned, was flung back against the coat rack beside the shattered front entrance.

The intruder rose to his feet but had difficulty acquiring his prey; he struggled with the night vision goggles that had been knocked askew by the impact, and in the dark he strained to gain a better view. Keene, on the other hand, had adjusted to the dark and saw quite well what loomed in front of him: a masked man with tactical gear, a Kevlar vest, a rifle, a pistol, and a knife. He only had a second to act before the assassin would be back in action.

Reaching back over his head for the only weapon available, Keene ripped the coat rack off the wall, the one that had previously held running shoes. Clenching it tightly in front of him, he lunged forward, prongs out toward the bastard who had been heading up to kill his wife.

"Aim high, there's Kevlar on his chest," he said to himself.

With a wet, crunching impact, he drove the rack across the face of the dark intruder, the only vulnerable area now that the goggles had been knocked askew. One of the hooks drove deep into an eye socket and the man went down with a convulsive shudder.

For the moment, all was silent. Keene scrambled over the prostrate, still moaning, and twitching body up the stairs to the room where Kaye breathed. He closed the door quietly behind him. It was dark as a tomb, a shocking juxtaposition to the recent chaos below and outside. Kaye still lay quietly, the suck and hiss of the ventilator providing the only offering to his senses. The cicadas were still mute. Apart from the throbbing tympany of his heart and the pain in his face, ear, and shoulder, that breathing machine sound was the only sensation in Keene's awareness.

Keene limped to the bedside. Suddenly, immediately behind him, the bedroom door burst open as angry voices in an unknown tongue barked out like hounds on the scent, braying their victory, their quarry treed. The doctor desperately threw his body across the soft blankets that covered his sleeping spouse, the last futile act of a man in love on the precipice of oblivion.

As he lunged toward the bed, he saw or felt himself sinking into the stinking black vapor that seemed to materialize all around and over his love. The darkness encased him and stung his skin from face to feet, a prickly, acidic sensation that seemed to be tearing the flesh from his bones. He felt that he was being burned alive.

"Oh JESUS, OH, JESUS," he wailed, saying the only thing he knew to say. He and his love had only seconds to live.

Suddenly a blinding flash blanketed the room, accompanied by a horrible compressing blast that squeezed the air out of his lungs and threatened to implode his skull. In a semiconscious daze, he pressed himself tighter against his wife and turned his head away from the direction of the intruders who had burst through the door. He did not desire to look death in the eye.

His head twisted in the direction of the back wall of the bedroom, which had previously showcased a frosted glass window whose panes were joined by antique lead. It was now gone, the ragged fragments of wood, lead, and glass framing the empty space. Looking beyond the window, Keene's blurry gaze took in the pasture and hillside that backed up to the property. And on top of the hill, he spied what looked like a man in a long robe. Still and upright, with hands raised.

Suddenly there were more flashes of light and shattering of glass. *POP POP POP*, then a staccato burst, and another.

His head split in another exploding flash. He felt his stunned body collapse and constrict, and it seemed to melt and merge into the Tuscany-themed quilt that covered his Kaye. "Oh, Jesus! Save us!!"

Another flash. He felt himself spinning into a vortex of unbearable light.

Darkness.

# AWAKE AGAIN (33 A.D.)

*Thump. Thump.* A gentle rhythm pushed against his cheek and rocked his head softly up and down. He felt gentle caresses across the top of his head, someone stroking his hair gently and picking shards of glass and splinters of wood out of it.

A soft voice said, "Hi, honey."

He couldn't open his eyes. This dream felt too real, too good …

"Look at me, baby. Do you know what's happening? I don't understand."

Keene found his view through half-closed lids. His head had come to rest atop Kaye's belly. The baby continued to beat a happy rhythm against his temple. His eyes opened tentatively, then melted into a countenance that he hadn't seen in a long time: a radiant face, blonde streaming hair, sparkling eyes. No face mask, no distress. And the hands that had just recently been barely able to move now channeled strong fingers through his hair. He felt a touch he had never thought he would feel again.

He started upright. Bits of plaster, splintered wood, and shards of glass sprinkled the floor, sparkling in the brilliant dawning sun that poured through the gaping frame where there once was a window.

"I—I don't know ..." Keene's bafflement deepened. He gazed unbelievingly into the face of his love. She showed no apparent signs of illness. Strong and vibrant. As he sat up, his attention was drawn to voices in the doorway and the abrasive sounds of things being dragged. He caught a glimpse of what appeared to be the receding legs and feet of some *body* being dragged down the stairs. A crimson trail was all that was left behind to mark the path.

A dark masked man in full tactical gear appeared briefly in the hall. Though the face was covered, the eyes and general posture of the man conveyed the joyful cockiness and swagger of a military man, a special operator fresh from "mission accomplished."

"Just chillax a bit right there, Doc. Everything's OK. We got this. Oh, by the way, you got a visitor. We figured we ought to let him in."

Keene slid himself up to the top of the bed. He embraced and was strongly embraced in return by the girl of his dreams. Her lithe and strong body rose against his as they held each other fast. Then Fred appeared at the door.

"Gee, Doc. You just had WWIII around here! Almost didn't get in but it seems one of the soldiers knew who I was. His mom used to be a patient at Emory, and while I was trying to fast-talk my way in, he overheard my story and said it was okay. Oh, and sorry I was late! Though maybe I wouldn't have been much help in all of this." He looked around at the general mayhem. "You look kinda beat up there, Doc. Hey! Is that a bullet hole in the back of your shoulder?"

Keene nodded. "I think it just grazed me, but have at it, Fred."

Fred laid hands on Keene's shoulder. Fred winced as the pain passed into his own. Keene was relieved of his.

"So where did you go off to?"

"You know, Doc, I told you that what we were both up against and trying to heal wasn't a physical problem. That's why I couldn't do much two days ago and it took me a little longer to figure it all out. It's another kind of warfare, Doc. It was a demon. I left to do a bit of investigating and to get a little counseling and to pray for guidance. I got it all right. But I didn't think I'd come back this morning to all this." His eyes again scanned the general destruction in the room.

"You know, when I was touching Kaye, I knew there was something evil. I could smell something I hadn't smelled in a long time. And it wasn't Granny's oatmeal cookies. It was foul. And I remembered something I hadn't remembered in a long time. That's what I had to go and check out yesterday.

"Doc, I wasn't entirely open about my past to you. But I was thinking about how you and me got together. And how I told you I got run out of town because everyone wanted the healing and not the healer. That wasn't exactly true. I never told you where I was from. Seems that you and me have a past. I'm from a little town up in the mountains, and when I was a teenager I worked on a cow farm for a guy named Chambers."

Keene was aghast, transfixed.

"There was this little kid named Danny who stayed in a cabin next door to the pasture where I helped tend the cows. And one day you discovered that dead calf down by the stream. But that little fella didn't just die. That little bull was sacrificed, Dr. Dan. It was bad. The guys who did it worked right there on the ranch with me. A bunch of them were just plain wicked folk. They came from old families in the mountains that used to run moonshine. Most of those families, more like gangs, moved on from there into drugs that got flown in from Mexico. Regular pipeline to the city.

"They knew I wasn't one of them. They called me preacher boy. Truth is that after I got out of school to come back to preach, they threatened to kill me. Would have, too, if I hadn't run off and changed my name. They have connections, y'know. They can track a person down anywhere.

"One of the guys on the farm was from a family named 'Poppell.' As it turns out, that's not the family's real name. It's 'Popov.' Russian. They changed it decades ago to blend in with country folk, but the ties to Russia remain. That's where the drug-running comes in. Russian mafia. Demon worship.

"That day when we burned that poor calf in the field, something strange happened. That wasn't any ordinary fire and smoke. I could feel it, and I bet you did, too. And that stench. It wasn't like any fire I've ever smelled before. But it was the same thing I smelled yesterday. Something came after you, Dr. Dan, didn't it? A long time ago. You hear people talk about guardian angels, right?" Keene nodded. "There's some on the other side, too. He, or it, has had its eye on you since that day, and it's been after you your whole life. I just figured all that out and was coming back here to do something about it. But it seems like you and the Lord, and whoa! a small army have taken care of all that."

"Well, Fred, you took care of the pain in my shoulder. But that … that black thing, that cloud. It's been following me … us … not just since medical school but my whole life? Where is it now?"

"I believe the Lord took care of that … it … of him. And you took care of a whole lot yourself! But in my digging I found out whatever this demon is or was. It has a name: Krivda. The name means 'crooked' in the Slavic dialect. Crooked as in deceptive, seeming like the 'truth' but really being quite the opposite. Anyway, I think it is gone now. At least I hope so ... well, I'm not totally sure. But you did good, kid!" Fred grinned a grin of deep relief and satisfaction.

Keene turned, leaned back on the bed, and snuggled close to Kaye, who had been listening with rapt, if somewhat baffled, attention.

"I love you," they said simultaneously.

✯✯✯

Later that day, Kaye gathered herself together, and Sally, Julie, and a few close friends helped her extricate herself and her things from the wreckage. They pampered her, washed and styled her hair, and arrayed her in lovely attire that she hadn't worn in a long time. They dismissed Daniel and told him to come back later. Workmen had already begun to arrive to clear up and repair the mess. Their demeanor and bearing betrayed the fact that these weren't ordinary craftsmen. They had the look of men who had a decidedly military skillset to augment their status as handymen.

From the street, the mansion and carriage house looked largely undisturbed, as the warzone was entirely restricted to the rear of the office, the back courtyard, and, especially, the carriage house. Peter Johnson and his wife, Patti, had come over, crossing the green space between their two houses. The path between them was well worn, as Daniel and Peter had gotten very close, spending many hours together over the months after the death of Stephen.

In the midst of the low hedgerow fence that separated their properties, Peter had constructed a "sheepgate," an exact reproduction of the gates that separated grazing properties in the Cotswolds of England. They had a circular design that housed a turnstile in the middle, allowing people to traverse the fence but keeping sheep from crossing.

During their visit, Peter and Patti had volunteered their guest quarters as accommodations for Daniel and Kaye while repairs to the carriage house were carried out. The Keenes were all too happy to accept.

Daniel strolled around the front of the mansion to find Fred and Pastor Jon, the coffee business owner, in deep conversation on the front porch, riding their respective Windsor rockers in unison. They were reviewing the events of the day and of the past months and years.

"I've got nothing but questions, guys," said Keene. "First of all, is it gone?"

"I was just asking Jon the same thing," replied Fred. "It seems he's had some experience with such things in the mission field."

"And what do you think?" asked Daniel.

"Well, as in other third-world countries, people in Central America are not so bound by the anti-supernatural presuppositions of the rest of us supposedly "advanced" nations. When we bring the Gospel to these people, we're always finding that there's a lot of work to do to free them from their demons. And don't misunderstand me. These beings are real. It's just that in our world, people deny their existence. In a way, it's much harder to get rid of demons here because people just aren't ready to embrace a "spiritual" experience.

"There, you present the truth of the Gospel. You don't usually have to mop up the demons, but when you do it's pretty straightforward."

"How do you do that?" Keene dug deeper.

"Well, pretty often you just have to call them by name and tell them to be gone by the power of the blood of Jesus."

"By name?"

"Yes," Jon replied. "Historically, and in all cultures, to name something or someone gives you power over them. And down there, just as in cultures all over the world, there are hundreds if not thousands of demons and entities that torment the populace and try to keep them from the truth."

"Speaking of truth, I told him about Krivda, Dr. Dan," said Fred. "I don't think it's any coincidence that our particular demon is bent (no pun intended) on portraying a 'crooked' version of what appears to be truth. We've had our share of discussions, haven't we? On how the entire world is caught up in lies, distorted versions of truth."

"I'll say," said Dan wryly.

"And you've spent your whole life seeking real truth. That's why you've been a 'prime target' all along."

# O.K. CORRAL (33 A.D.)

Keene and his wife, now restored, glowing with health and strength, walked arm in arm down the path that connected their home to the Johnsons'. He carried an overstuffed carpet bag that transported enough clothing and personal items to get them through a few days in exile from their wrecked abode. After Kaye's friends had finished fussing over her, they had spent the day sifting through the rubble to gather up what they needed and to take stock of what would be required for Keene and Kaye to get back to normal. All the while, they were sidestepping dozens of young men and women, who, though they were obviously members of some law enforcement or government team, wore no insignia nor bore any outward evidence of whatever branch they worked for. Keene likened them to a bunch of human "unmarked cars."

Darkness was descending. The last glow of the day lingered in the sky. Hundreds of low clouds scuttered across the deep blue canopy of the approaching night, alternately revealing and then hiding the rays of the rising near-full moon. The clouds cast fleeting shadows that appeared and disappeared in quick succession. A stiff breeze stirred the oak trees that lined the property and mussed Kaye's hair.

Keene, ever the weather watcher, spoke. "Honey, go on ahead. I'm gonna take a look at this weather. Got this app on my phone to look at the radar." He gestured in the direction of the Johnsons' house where Peter and Patti stood, beckoning on the veranda at the side of their antebellum home. She obliged, not being fond of high winds. Traces of her Oklahoma heritage contributed to an innate fear of storms. She had always wanted to live in a house that featured a "frady-hole" in it, as Uncle Dave called it, to escape approaching whirlwinds.

Daniel waved to the Johnsons as Kaye accompanied them into the shelter of the house. He turned to survey the lowering sky and the clouds that advanced in aggressive waves toward him. There was something different about this weather.

In this part of Georgia, he mused, bad weather invariably approached from the Southwest, driven by rapidly moving cold fronts that pushed sometimes violent squall lines from Alabama into the Peach State. These clouds and the wind that propelled them were advancing from the Northeast. Highly unusual.

Keene looked down at the radar app on his cellphone to see if there was any evidence of severe weather on the screen. Startled, he saw that there was absolutely nothing to see. He checked another weather app. Nothing there either. He looked back again at the sky that continued to descend upon him.

Then, in the center of the line of racing clouds, he saw it: a singular dark shape, a spinning cloud that separated itself from the others and came lower, approaching as a black jet liner heading toward touchdown on the runway, only this runway was the path and sheepgate where Keene stood.

More mysteriously, though the wind was rising, there was no sound as there usually was with thunderstorms and tornadoes. Instead, an eerie and suffocating silence permeated the atmosphere. The black vortex spun ever closer.

Suddenly Keene's mind was overcome with a vision, or multiple visions all at once: of a small boy recoiling at the sight and smell of a mutilated calf; of hiding on the back porch of a mountain cabin from the foul black cloud that surrounded the place; of a young man struggling under the bedcovers to block out the vision of tornadoes in a bad dream; of that same young man lying paralyzed in a dorm room bed as a foul black presence filled his room. He could see and feel all at once in his mind's eye the smoky black presence that accompanied and surrounded the Russian healer lady, the doctors in the pain clinic, the college philosophy professor, and the pharmaceutical company executive who had acted so inappropriately toward his wife. Most of all, the misty, swirling dark presence that had encased his sweetheart and he had dived into in desperation the night before loomed ominously in his brain. A familiar foul burning and rotting stench filled his nostrils.

But instead of fear, a grim determination flooded Keene's soul. He faced the inky, reeking cloud. He remembered his conversation with Fred and Jon that afternoon. He knew once and for all what or who this was that threatened him.

He shouted into the silent wind. "I know who you are! You are Krivda! Crooked, Deceiver, servant of Satan. You have permeated the world with your lies. But I know the Truth and the Truth has set me free!"

The cloud stopped as if running into a clear glass barrier, the spinning strands of cloud and smoke, like the tentacles of an octopus, dispersed and dissipated against the invisible wall, spreading in every direction except toward the doctor.

"In the name of the Lord Jesus and by the power of His blood, I rebuke you and command you: Begone and never return again!"

And it was. Gone.

All the clouds disappeared and the moon shone brightly as it inched higher above the horizon. The dusk surrendered to the darkening night. All was quiet and at peace. Keene embraced the victory once and for all.

# RETRIBUTION (33 A.D.)

Hassan backed his refrigerated tractor trailer expertly up to the loading dock. He had been promoted to a much more important task in the delivery system. The refrigerated cargo in this truck came straight from the manufacturer and was now on the threshold of a national distribution hub. He carried vaccines. Dozens of smaller trucks would soon be carrying this cargo to other smaller local and regional distribution hubs. From there they would be distributed to hospitals and pharmacies.

As he exited the truck, he found himself surrounded by no fewer than a dozen men and women wearing blue parkas. Emblazoned on the front and across the back of their uniforms were the letters "FBI."

✡✡✡

In a government building in Silver Springs, Maryland, an IT technician sat in front of an impressive array of screens. He and the others in the massive room monitored myriad data streams that flowed into the FDA from all over the country and the world, including input from the VAERS (Vaccine Adverse Event Reporting System). He felt a hand on his shoulder and turned to face three blue-clad and stern-faced gentlemen.

"Sir, would you please come with us?"

✭✭✭

Simultaneously, in Worcester, Massachusetts and Pelzer, South Carolina, the last of hundreds of employees at pharmaceutical manufacturing plants marched stiffly from the facilities, escorted by dozens of the same blue-clad officers. Locks, yellow tape, and armed guards prevented reentry to the buildings.

✭✭✭

Similarly, in a Manhattan skyscraper's upper-level executive suites and offices, more blue-clad and neatly suited men and women spread over the premises. They politely requested that the offices' occupants return to their homes and prepare for a long vacation.

Several inhabitants of the building were not leaving unaccompanied. One was a handsome man in an expertly tailored suit. His hands were in zip ties behind his back.

✭✭✭

On the top floor of a sleek, modern, glassy building in Brussels, a portly man in his eighties, clad in a tailored suit, sat behind his desk. He drummed his fingers on the polished surface. A cellphone lay within easy reach. He had been expecting a call for days.

He turned his chair and looked out over the skyline, drawing a deep, impatient breath. The sun had gone down hours ago and it was well after midnight. All the employees had gone home, even the hard workers who wished to curry favor by demonstrating their endurance into the late hours. The only remaining personnel were a few janitors and security guards. They had made their rounds already on this floor and had gone on to other levels. The gentleman was all alone.

He rose from his leather chair and began to pace along the breadth of the office, again casting his gaze across the city. He held the cellphone in his hand, alternately staring at the blank and silent screen, and then reaching hesitantly as if to dial a number. His preoccupation with the phone and the call that wasn't coming was interrupted by the sound of someone at his door.

"Who's there?" he shouted with no small amount of exasperation in his voice.

The door opened slowly, and two black-clad figures slipped in quietly. The gentleman, indignant at the intrusion, said again, "Who are you? What is the meaning of this?"

The only answer he received was the muffled report of suppressed pistol shots.

# NEWSFLASH (33 A.D.)

It had been barely more than forty-eight hours since the attack, and already there were scarcely any signs of the havoc that had played out. Keene crouched on the carriage house steps, coffee cup in hand, surveying his surroundings, the courtyard, the wisteria-covered slate path. The freshly planted pansies lined up (a bit too much like soldiers, Kaye would say) along it.

The smell of newly sawn wood, paint, and primer filled the air. At least a dozen sober-faced, athletic young men in utility attire, armed to the teeth (with gardening or woodworking tools) scurried busily about. One carried a hand-hewn walnut bench up the porch and into the foyer. It was an exact copy of the fragmented one that another man was tossing into the dumpster bin.

"This goes here, right, Doc?"

"Yeah, right there below the banister against that wall."

"Okay. Hey, Doc! I thought you got shot in the shoulder?"

"Oh, that? It was just a spatter from somewhere else."

"Yeah, right," the soldier acquiesced in a skeptical manner and returned to his task. He had been the first one to encounter Keene on the explosive night. He was the one to sound the "all clear" to Keene as Keene sat stunned and bewildered at Kaye's bedside. He had seen the wound.

Keene's eyes roamed up to the back door of the main house and the attached utility shed. A neatly manicured mound of moss surrounded by smooth white river stones marked the resting place of the shed's recent occupant. The local radio station streamed its morning newscast through the app on his cellphone.

"This is a CBS live special report. Federal agents of the ATF, Homeland Security, and the FBI carried out an early-morning raid on the Manhattan offices of Pelzer Pharma. Officials seized files and hard drives and took a number of employees into custody. Among those arrested, handcuffed, and removed from the headquarters was Chief Operating Officer Johannes Akhtar. Akhtar, known in the industry as one of the most brilliant executives in the entire pharma world, is widely credited with the resounding success of Pelzer's research and development programs, most notably with vaccines. Under his guidance, Pelzer took the lead in ending the recent worldwide viral pandemic via innovative vaccine development. The company was promising to protect the world from future pandemics with their newest offering, Panacea, causing the market value of Pelzer Pharm as a whole to soar over thirty percent in the last year. Pelzer and the FDA have just released news of the suspension of the release of this new vaccine, and the New York Stock Exchange has announced a freeze on the trading of Pelzer shares. Sources within the FBI and other agencies are not shedding any light on today's events.

"In other news from the top circles of power and industry in the world, this special report has come in from Brussels, Belgium. Chaos erupted in the executive suites of the Global

Financial Council last night. Masked gunmen entered the building, breached security, and invaded the headquarters of this organization of the world's financial elite. There have been reports of gunfire and one casualty, the organization's head, Hans Schultz, who was slain in his office. It is unknown currently if any group claims responsibility for what appears to be a terrorist attack that bears all the marks of a specifically targeted assassination."

Keene clicked off the phone and ambled up the slate stones to the back of the office. A swag of wisteria caressed his shoulder as he maneuvered underneath the arched trellis. Looking through the fresh panes of the newly repaired back door, Keene could spy his sweetheart sitting in the waiting area of the office. Resplendent and radiant in the full bloom of pregnancy, her face aglow and eyes dancing with joy (as her pretty feet already were), she held court with a few of her closest friends. Annie sat close beside her at the center. They whispered and giggled, joyfully and tearfully anticipating and planning the baby shower that was coming together at lightning speed.

Keene chose the safe route away from the gaggle and rounded the alley side of the mansion to take another survey of the ground and the street. Even the most observant busybody, viewing the office from the street, would not have been able to tell that a war had been fought in this place over the weekend. And though word of the "home invasion" (as the story was told through town) quickly spread, it appeared that the real story was successfully hidden.

Casting his view to the street, Keene was half startled to see two government-issue black SUVs swoop briskly to a stop in front of the office. He could make out the now-familiar faces of the driver and passenger in the front of the first car.

They were the same "real estate" guys who had been casing his joint. A brief text message on Keene's phone immediately after the Battle of Madison (as he called it) had informed him these guys were "friendlies." He could not make out the occupants of the second vehicle through its darkly tinted windows.

The back door of the second SUV opened. A well-put-together gentleman in his forties stepped briskly onto the sidewalk and strode confidently, if not also somewhat eagerly, up the path to greet Keene. His face reflected both joy and sternness, the countenance of a man accustomed to dealing with crisis and hardship, able to handle victory or defeat with a sanguine equanimity.

It was Special Agent in Charge John Ward.

"Dr. Keene!" he extended his hand toward the doctor, who, grasping it firmly in return, noted the "Semper Fi" tattoo inscribed along the agent's muscular forearm.

"So glad we're meeting like this! Ya mind if we walk and talk? A lot has been going down. I want to answer your questions as much as I can. You do deserve it, since, well, I'll explain in a minute. And I'm really wanting to apologize that you were kept in the dark for so long, but it was really necessary for you to think I was blowing you off when we talked before. There was way too much at stake. Oh, and I thought you might want a little extra company on our stroll."

At that point, the passenger-side back door of the SUV opened. Out stepped Master Sergeant Sally Anderson and Professor Alfonzo.

"What the heck?" Keene thought to himself, and he shook his head in disbelief.

"I told you I knew some guys, didn't I?" Sally grinned that sly, secret grin again. "Well, remember that crew member of mine who was so eager to inspect my ass, after my 9mm plugging on that rooftop in Algiers?"

"You said Morocco." Keene laughed.

"Whatever, well, this is my Jackie-boy. And the professor, here. That's another story. Jackie, wanna explain?"

"Well, Doc, again I'm sorry that I had to act like I was blowing you off when you called me. But you see, I've known the professor a long time. He called me right after he saw you. It's his job to think about worst case scenarios, and though you told him you were just writing a book, your theory was spot on.

"The professor here is, for the record, retired. But in the 'community,' no one is ever really retired. As I said, the professor began to investigate the possibility that the scenario you talked about could be put into action. He still has contacts in intelligence agencies in Great Britain and all over Europe, even on the other side of the fence, you might say. What I'm about to tell you is classified, you understand?"

Keene nodded.

"The professor insisted that all available resources be directed to checking out your theory. A lot of people began operations immediately: Interpol, MI6, Mossad, the FBI, the CIA, and Homeland. All I can say, Doc, is you were right."

"How did you connect the dots?"

"It was pretty obvious there was only one man at the top of a pharmaceutical supply chain who could possibly coordinate something like this."

"Akhtar," Keene said.

"Correct. So, we began monitoring communications between Akhtar and his people and other places. We picked up connections with distribution centers and couriers. We looked into employees at the FDA who had worked at Pelzer and might have had close contact with Akhtar; found a few.

"Of all the places in the world that a guy would pick to experiment on a poison plan, it happened to be your backyard. You were the only one to make a fuss about it and be persistent. Sally told me how you see, hear, and feel things most people do not. Hell, if you didn't, if you hadn't, things in the whole world would be fixin' to look a whole lot different a month or two from now. And by the way, we nabbed a few jackasses at the FDA, and even, unfortunately, in my own house."

"What about the China connection?" Keene asked.

Alfonzo spoke up. "We were watching Akhtar's communications through Iran. We also knew he was getting assistance from other places."

"Like where? Who?"

Alfonzo hesitated. "Let's just say a strong European money man."

"You mean like that Nazi Schultz guy? The one who was just murdered by terrorists?"

Alfonzo did not answer. Keene speculated to himself things in Europe might have been handled differently from the way they are on US soil.

"So, Doc," Ward said, breaking the awkward silence, "you won't be hearing from us anymore. None of this happened, y'know? News media is getting their story about the little brouhaha around this place. Other stuff in other places? That's covered, too. So, you'll be getting no credit here for saving the world, Doc." He smiled broadly.

Sally angled over next to Keene and gave him a side hug as they walked. "Thanks, Doc, for being you. For healing me, and for miracles that I'll never understand. And hey, I see the biggest one waving at you over there." She slid back into the SUV and nodded toward the office as the door shut. On the front porch of the mansion stood a rapturous vision. Sweet

Kaye, surrounded by her entourage, beckoning him to come to her.

# EPILOGUE

It had now been two weeks since that violent and supernatural night. The local news had been abuzz about the mysterious home and office invasion of the small-town doctor. Contradictory and totally fictitious testimonies regarding mayhem, gunfights, pyrotechnics, a struggle, and blood saturated the media. Most strange and unexplainable of all was the irrefutable fact that the invaders and those who battled them had vanished into thin air. Keene, of course, pled total ignorance, having been unconscious, he explained, and not remembering anything about the incident. But there was more in the story still. There was the miraculous healing of the doctor's pregnant and supposedly dying wife.

Keene sat once again on the steps of the carriage house porch. Kaye, in fact, was again sitting in the reception area of the office, surrounded by adoring and still astounded friends and church members as they celebrated the new life, both of them, with a shower of gifts and praises for the miracle they had witnessed.

Keene stepped along the slate under the wisteria. He picked up a shard of glass that had been overlooked. He recognized the frosted pattern as coming from the glazed transom above their bedroom door. How had it gotten so far out in the courtyard? "Stupid question," he thought.

He rubbed the sore spot above his ear, recalling the searing pain and the flashes of light. That last flash before the darkness had been decidedly different than all the others. And Kaye had been healed. He suspected he knew the truth of what had transpired. Was it a sudden release of healing energy from his own body? Or was it a miracle? He savored the satisfaction of his final confrontation with the evil presence, but he knew the credit was not his to claim.

His gaze passed from the spot in the grass where the glass fragment had lain to that small mound of earth near the ivy-covered back wall of the office, the spot where Tigger had been buried. Her bowl and collar rested on the top of the mound. She remained the only visible casualty of that night.

For a frantic moment, Keene firmly but lovingly rebuffed the attention of a new three-month-old boxer puppy. A whirling dervish, she was bouncy and dangerously affectionate. "Down, Roo! No, Roo!" This was going to take some work, but he loved her. Her official AKC name was "Ruby Star," or Roo for short. After all, who was even more bouncy than Tigger? Roo, of course.

"How did I get back to this, Danny?" Kaye gestured downward at her restored and very pregnant body as she also did a little dog-dodging. "Was it you? Or Jesus?"

"I don't know. Both, I guess?"

The running shoes hung once again with eager anticipation by the door.

# ABOUT THE AUTHOR

Dr. David Kunz owns and runs the family practice he established in 1988 outside of Atlanta, Georgia after attending Wake Forest University and Emory University School of Medicine, serving seven years in the Navy, and completing his residency at the Naval Regional Medical Center in Charleston, South Carolina.

He spent forty-two wonderful years with his wife before her passing in 2022 and is the proud father and grandfather to four children and four grandchildren. He has always been a writer, mostly essays, stories, commentaries, poems, and satire. In addition to writing, Dr. Kunz also enjoys singing and playing guitar, cycling, swimming, and other physical activities.

Made in the USA
Columbia, SC
30 October 2024